FINAL
NOTICE

JOE GORES

DOVER PUBLICATIONS, INC.
Mineola, New York

Copyright

Bibliographical Note

This Dover edition, first published in 2019, is an unabridged republication of the work originally published by Random House, Inc., New York, in 1973. This edition includes "File #10: The Maimed and the Halt," which was originally published in *Ellery Queen's Mystery Magazine* in January 1976. Readers should be forewarned that the text contains racial and cultural references of the era in which it was written and may be deemed offensive by today's standards.

Library of Congress Cataloging-in-Publication Data

Names: Gores, Joe, 1931–2011, author.
Title: Final notice : a DKA File novel / Joe Gores.
Description: Dover edition. | Mineola, New York : Dover Publications, Inc., 2019. | Series: A DKA File novel
Identifiers: LCCN 2019014196 | ISBN 9780486838311 | ISBN 0486838315
Subjects: | GSAFD: Mystery fiction.
Classification: LCC PS3557.O75 F56 2019 | DDC 813/.54—dc23
LC record available at https://lccn.loc.gov/2019014196

Manufactured in the United States by LSC Communications
83831501
www.doverpublications.com

2 4 6 8 10 9 7 5 3 1

2019

for Rog
because he let me kill him twice
once by water, once in blood

Contents

FINAL
NOTICE

One

SHE WAS a willowy girl wearing a skirt that was too short. At first glance her face held so much vivacity that Ballard thought she was feverish. Then he realized the glitter of her eyes came from contact lenses.

"I represent California Citizens Bank, Mrs. Schilling, and—"

"I don't know anything about it and I don't want to know anything about it," she snapped. With the expectancy gone from her face, she was just a skinny woman showing too much skinny leg from behind a realty-office desk.

"Your name is on the contract."

"I don't care whose name is on what, I told the other man from your company that the Bastard has the car." She said "the Bastard" as if it were her husband's legal name. "Get out of here. Leave me alone."

Ballard had just gotten the case on the 1972 Duster that day, because the man assigned to it had been unable to do anything with Mrs. Schilling.

"Your name's on the contract."

"Leave me alone!" she shrieked.

A bald head was stuck around the edge of the interior door that led to the other office of the suite.

"Trouble, Joanne?" it asked.

Ballard sighed. "No trouble. I'm just leaving."

The features assembled under the bald dome glared at him for a moment longer, then were withdrawn. Joanne Schilling's mouth moved in triumph, as if she wanted to laugh and spit at the same time.

Ballard was feeling a lot of sympathy for the Bastard. He paused in the outside doorway.

"I hope you remember I gave you a chance to cooperate when the bank socks you with a grand-theft warrant."

Her mouth stopped moving. Her face became somber, then sullen. "Is that on the level? Can they do that?"

Ballard didn't say anything. It was a trick he had learned from Dan Kearny. Make them come to you. It worked. An unexpected flush spread over her cheeks.

"The Bastard is sleeping with some . . . some spade chick." Jarred past that admission, she was suddenly eager to cooperate. "She lives down south of Market in a little park-sort-of-area. South . . . South-something. I went down there once just . . . to see . . ."

"South Park?" asked Ballard, whose knowledge of the city was becoming mildly encyclopedic.

"That's it! South Park."

Since the Bastard's given work address was on Howard Street, Ballard swung over to check it out on the way to South Park. It was early enough in the month so he could give a couple of consecutive hours to the Schilling Duster, especially after reading the crappy report written on it. He didn't blame the client for yelling.

Avery Printing had the second floor of an old concrete building from before the '06 quake which had been tricked out with new aluminum-sash windows and a vestibule with lots of nonfuctional glass. The thump and roar of presses filled Avery's little reception area. The pudgy girl working the electric typewriter had dandruff, and pimples on her chin.

"Gee, Mr. Schilling doesn't really *work* here, he just sort of . . ." She looked beyond Ballard and brightened. "Oh! Mr. Avery . . ."

Avery was a heavy man in wash pants. Dark hair sprouted at the open neck of his white shirt. He had a smear of ink up one hairy forearm, and kept turning over Ballard's Daniel Kearny Associates card (Branch Offices Throughout California, Affiliates in All Major American Cities) with blunt fingers while listening to Ballard's pitch.

"Yeah, well, I know Bob Schilling, all right. Thing is, he's a sort of jobber, you get me?"

"No," Ballard admitted.

"He gets printing jobs around town, then farms 'em out to small presses like us. Funny you wouldn't know, being a friend of his . . ."

"I'm just trying to buy his car. I only met the man once."

"Yeah, well, I'll tell him you was by when he comes in next."

Ballard walked back to his car, a tall, well-conditioned blondish man in his mid-twenties, wearing a suit but no topcoat in San Francisco's mild mid-October sunshine. He wrote notes on the pink report carbon stapled face-out to the back of the Schilling assignment sheet, started to stick it up over the visor ready for a report, then remembered he still had South Park to check out.

In the 1860s South Park, designed by an Englishman some ten years earlier as a copy of London's Berkeley Square, was the residence of those wealthy and influential Southern gentlemen known as the Copperheads because of their virulent opposition to abolition. A century later, by one of those ironies of time, it had become an exclusively black slum.

Not that Ballard knew any of this as he turned off Third Street. Driving slowly around the one-way oval of South Park Avenue, looking for the Duster, he thought only that it must have been a nice residential area once and that it was a pity industry had grown up around and in it.

In the center of the startlingly green mini-park/playground, four blacks sat at one of the tables having lunch. At the far end of the oval, a one-legged black man wearing a GIANTS baseball cap crutched his way from the Home Market with a bottle of wine in a paper bag.

The houses were old, weathered, with false fronts like the houses in western movies, except they were painted unexpectedly bright—if faded—colors. New paint couldn't hide the age of the Hotel Madrid.

In a garage with the overhead door up, four middle-aged black men and two equally middle-aged black women were playing poker. An obvious whore drifted like a tattered butterfly from the Yellowrose Hotel, 84 Rooms, Day or Week. Ma and Pa businesses alternated with the houses or occupied their ground floors.

But no Duster.

Ballard pulled into the yellow zone in front of a *For Lease* import company to note that fact on the assignment sheet and sort through his other cases. Parked directly in front of his Plymouth was an immensely bright, immensely shiny 1973 Cadillac convertible with the top down. Fire-engine red. License 333 FFX.

An elegantly slim Caucasian, the first besides himself Ballard had seen in South Park, strolled up to the Cadillac and got in. He moved like an athlete. He had beautifully wavy hair and the most exquisite tailoring Ballard had ever seen.

Neither the suit nor the Cadillac fit the neighborhood.

Come back tomorrow morning about three-thirty, Ballard thought. Schilling and his lady love would be home by then even if they'd been bar-hopping with coffee afterward. He could use an easy repo, he'd knocked off only five cars since the first of the month. O'Bannon, the old pro, had already chalked up twelve on the Monthly Work Breakdown board.

The man was getting out of the Caddy again. 333 FFX. Something flickered in the back of Ballard's mind. He began searching through the *Active* files from his attaché case as the elegant man walked by him again. Three 3s in the license. Older than he had looked from the back, a good ten years older than Ballard. Thin features almost classically handsome, clean-shaven, with a wide firm mouth—only the eyes betrayed his age. Dark eyes that should have been Latin and liquid, but instead were like alcohol on the skin. Ice eyes, without depths.

Three 3s on the license plate? Not in his *Active* files. But dammit, Ballard had *seen,* somewhere . . . *Skip* list? This carried license numbers only, and only for the hot ones: cars driven by dead skips, embezzlers, absconders, out-and-out thieves. Every field agent's dream was to knock one off the skip list. In three years with DKA, Ballard never had.

Nothing with three 3s. But dammit . . .

He suddenly grabbed the mike clipped to the dash, flipped on the radio and waited while it *squeerged* through warm-up. Office. That morning. Snooping O'Bannon's *In* box, as they all did to see what assignments the others were getting.

"SF-6 calling KDM 366 Control."

The voice of Kathy Onoda, DKA's Japanese office manager, said, "This is KDM 366. Go ahead, SF-6."

"Kathy, will you check O'B's *In* box and tell me if he's got an assignment on a 3-3-3-F-F-X?"

"10-4. Checking, Larry."

Ballard sat with the mike in his hand. It wouldn't be the right car, of course. This sort of thing happened to Kearny or O'B or even old Ed Dorsey, but never to . . .

"That's 3-3-3-F-F-X, a seventy-three Cad convert. Instructions . . ." Her voice thinned with excitement. "REPOSSESS ON SIGHT! *Go gettem Bears!*"

This was it. That always intense excitement, almost pure joy, when you faced the moment of action. Get out hot wire and pop keys. Lock up the Plymouth. Walk casually, as casually as the hard-eyed man had walked. No need for window picks, since the top was down.

He pushed over the four little sateen pillows on the seat, slid in, began working with his set of filed-down keys, gently, gingerly, always exerting the slightest sideways pressure, checking the rear-view mirror for trouble. He hadn't forgotten those eyes.

The key suddenly turned in his hand with that always unexpected ease, the radio came alive with classical music from KKHI, the starter gave a discreet stutter.

God*damn*, he had it! Even Kearny would have to admire this one. As he swung left into Second, a white-haired dumpy old woman ran off the curb waving her hands. He accelerated, just stifling the exuberant urge to give her the finger. God*damn!* Neat and nasty, and best of all, would be rubbing O'B's nose in it tonight, when the red-headed investigator got back from working Marin County.

Stopped by the light at Sixth, Ballard opened the glove box. Empty except for the Owner's Manual. No personal property apart from the sateen pillows and an incongruous comic book on the front seat. He riffled the pages.

The light changed. The cars behind the Caddy started honking. Ballard was staring at the comic book, open-mouthed.

Interlarded between the four-color pages were crisp new hundred-dollar bills.

Two

HONEYED DIXIE tones, rich with sexual implication, were coming from the office at the end of the hall.

"Shugah, you don't *know* what lovin' means until youah've had *me!*"

Bart Heslip, lounged in his chair and listening with one knee cocked against the edge of the desk, abruptly turned almost plum-black features toward the open door. At the far end of the hall, Larry Ballard was just topping the interior stairs of the old converted Victorian. It had once been a specialty whorehouse; now it was the head offices of DKA.

"Baby, Ah *heard* you were, why do you think Ah called youah up?" A very faint sheen of perspiration dotted the upper lip of the girl on the phone. She exclaimed delightedly, "Shugah, youah pick the spot . . ."

Ballard paused in the open doorway, eyebrows raised in question. Heslip waggled his own.

"Fifty dollahs foah all night, lovah," crooned the girl on the phone. She gave a low throaty laugh that sent a chill down the spines of both detectives. "Aftah one night with little ole *me,* shugah, youah going to want it *every* night. Eight o'clock? Phone booth behind the old Ocean Beach Amusement Pahk? Lovah, youah not . . ." She paused, gave the throaty laugh again. "Fahve-fouah and blond all *ovah,* baby. All right. Tonight. Ah can hardly wait."

She lowered the receiver very gently, then clapped her hands explosively and spun her swivel chair toward Heslip with a hard joyous laugh totally unlike her earlier tone.

"*Got* that son of a bitch!" she exclaimed.

"Buddha Head strikes again," said Heslip.

Kathy Onoda was an angular twenty-eight, Heslip's age, her almost classical Japanese features refined by illness and framed in a lustrous mane of gleaming jet hair. Not ill, she kept insisting, just run-down. Maybe so: office manager of DKA while raising two doll-like daughters and supporting a dead-beat husband who never seemed to graduate from Cal Berkeley.

"I just got here for the cartoon," said Ballard. "Who?"

"Gondolph," said Heslip.

"No shit? Beautiful! Want help tonight?"

Alex Gondolph had embezzled $7,000 from Fidelity Trust; Dan Kearny had given the assignment exclusively to Bart Heslip five days before, and had given the ex-professional boxer a week to turn him.

"Sure. I'll show you how it's done."

"You cats have all the fun," complained Kathy. She looked at Ballard. "What happened on that Caddy convert?"

With a dramatic flourish he laid five one-hundred-dollar bills on the desk. Heslip's eyes popped open. The black detective's sloping breadth of shoulder and depth of chest made him seem heavier than his 158 pounds. He had been with DKA for six years.

"Man, what—"

"Not payments. Personal property. The Caddy's in the barn."

"I have a feeling you'd better tell the Great White Father all about it," said Kathy weakly. "He's down in his cubbyhole."

"You walked into the middle of a payoff," rumbled Dan Kearny. He was a graying compact man in his mid-forties, with gray eyes turned bleak by over a quarter of a century spent probing the underbelly of society. "What's the name on the file?"

"Chandra."

"Chandra what?"

"Just Chandra. It came in that way from the client—Kathy checked it. I don't even know if it's a man or a woman."

"Sounds sort of exotic," mused Bart Heslip. Teeth flashed in his dark face; he seemed totally recovered from the concussion of half a year before. "Like a belly dancer or something. Swirling veils—"

"Swirling hundred-dollar bills." Kearny reached forward to shake a Lucky from the pack on his desk. He frowned at Ballard through the first cloud of smoke. "Write the money up as personal property, same as a box of tools in the trunk or something. Then we'll play it by ear." He changed subjects by looking back at Heslip. "I hear Kathy smoked out Gondolph."

"It was beautiful, Dan! Bartender in that joint on Eddy Street said Gondolph can only make it with little blond cuddly southern whores. So Kathy just laid it all over the Tenderloin that she's little and blond and cuddly, in a Dixie accent you gotta use a spoon on, and this afternoon she got his phone number."

"You and Larry are both going on it tonight?"

Heslip nodded.

Kearny scratched his massively pugnacious jaw. "Good. Fidelity's bonding company wriggled out from under on a technicality, and I want to do a good job for them. Use the old citizen's-arrest line: he's got to hand the money over to you tonight and show up at Fidelity in the morning, or blah blah blah."

"If he kicks up rough?"

"Then take him in, you're legal rep for Fidelity—but that's the last resort." He stubbed out his cigarette. He said to Ballard, "What are you doing on that Schilling car? The client's raising hell."

"The wife tells me he's got a girl friend down in South Park. That's how I spotted the Chandra Caddy."

"Keep after it."

Through the one-way glass door of his cubbyhole, Kearny watched them cross the garage to the field-agent cubicles against the far wall. He lit another cigarette.

Chandra. A damned odd one even to someone like him who'd started out knocking off cars for old man Walters down in L.A. as a teenager, five bucks a repo and pay your own transportation. Kearny had ridden out on a bicycle to grab his first hot car. Worked up to general manager of Walter's Auto Detectives after the war, quit in 1964 to start Daniel Kearny Associates.

He shook his head, remembering. O'Bannon in the field, teenage Kathy Onoda to answer the single telephone and set up files and skip-trace, Kearny to do all of those and hustle clients besides. Now DKA had nine California offices and a dozen field men in the Bay Area alone.

On sudden impulse, he jabbed the intercom button. In a moment Kathy's voice came through from the clerical offices above.

"Who's the client on that convertible Ballard just grabbed?"

"Golden Gate Trust, Dan. Pete Gilmartin."

He replaced the receiver, stabbed the button for an outside line, picked up, dialed the new assistant vice-president in charge of auto contracts at Golden Gate.

"Pete? Dan Kearny, how's it going? Listen, we've got that Caddy for you . . . Yeah, *damned* fast. Larry Ballard, one of our best men. Pete, what can you tell me about this Chandra . . ."

"Chandra is a dancer, has her own studio up in North Beach—on Grant at the corner of Edith Alley, I think it is," said Ed Dorsey.

He came into Ballard's already crowded cubicle. There was damned little about San Francisco old Ed didn't know; could give you cross streets for almost every hundred-block in the city. Past sixty, a white-haired, bumbling man wearing a topcoat and a snap-brim hat that took ten years off his age. He'd made and lost two sizable fortunes on the Pacific Coast Stock Exchange in his day.

Heslip tipped Ballard a wink. He didn't dig old Ed too much. Rough as a cob on the phone, mush out in the field where it counted.

"Say, Ed, we're going out after an embezzler tonight. Might get a bit sticky, man, we could sure use some extra muscle."

"Tonight?" Dorsey had a pink face getting jowly, weak watery blue eyes lent bogus authority by stern-rimmed glasses. "Dammit! Any other night, men, I'd be right out there with you. But . . . ah . . . I've got a meet set up tonight myself."

When he was gone, Heslip snickered softly. "If his wife'll let him out alone after dark."

They finished their reports a little before six, then walked down two blocks for Red Hot Doggies that somebody hadn't left in the infra-red oven long enough. A little after six, with the rush-hour traffic well thinned downtown, they rescued Ballard's car from South Park and left it by the DKA office.

Six-fifty. Time for Alex Gondolph, embezzler. Both investigators tensing up and hiding it from the other. They'd both been threatened numerous times with everything from razors to shotguns to vehicular homicide, but embezzlers *knew* they faced a possible felony rap if somebody caught up with them. And the last time DKA had gone looking for an embezzler, Heslip had ended up in a coma . . .

"Schilling ought to park that Duster in South Park after the bars close," said Ballard, just to be using his mouth. He shot a look at Heslip, so cool behind the wheel. Maybe forty pro fights taught you to mask it all, so the other cat in the ring with you would never know what was going on in your head.

Heslip yawned. "If his old lady was telling the truth. We'll take a look after we keep Kathy's date with Gondolph."

They drove out through the Richmond District that flanked that side of the park, then dropped over the steep incline to Forty-eighth Avenue and the Great Highway. Street lights by turns illuminated and dropped into shadow Ballard's unmemorably attractive features. Only unexpectedly watchful eyes lent the face distinction. He kept talking to quell the butterflies in his gut.

"You tell Corinne we were going after this cat tonight?"

"No. Hell, you know how she is, Larry. She just doesn't like detecting, period. And since I was in the hospital . . ."

"What's going to happen when you marry her?"

"One of us is gonna have to give, and it ain't gonna be me." The Great Highway was split to pass on either side of the several acres of blacktop parking that Playland at the Beach had once needed. Heslip parked. He amended, "Damned if I know what's gonna happen."

The insistent sea wind slapped at them with salty hands. Seven-forty. Time to kill, so they crossed the highway to stand by the concrete sea wall and stare out at the dimly rolling breakers.

"Tide's out," said Ballard.

Heslip shivered. Both men wore topcoats, but the wind cut through the unlined gabardines. "Hope I recognize the mother when I see him," he said unexpectedly.

"I doubt if there'll be one whole hell of a lot of guys standing around that phone booth."

"You don't think he'd be packing a gun?" asked Heslip even more unexpectedly. Before Ballard could reply, he answered himself, "Naw. No way. What time?"

"Eight minutes."

"Yeah."

Fronting the Great Highway was Playland, nearly dead, awaiting the high-rise development that would make it yet another memory in a city that lived on them. The only places still open were a pie shop, a Mexican café, and a pinball emporium. They went by the lank-haired groups of oriental teenagers desultorily *spronging* pinball machines, out the back door into the darkened midway and turned left, past a shivering sailor and his girl. The pay phone was at the far end by the old streetcar turn-around.

Ballard stopped to light a cigarette he didn't want so he could ask, "Is that him?"

By the booth was a short and rather tubby man. He had a round face and horn-rims and ears that stuck out from his head like clenched baby's fists. No overcoat. Double-knit suit of a rather electric-yellow even in that dim light. It fit him the way the skin fits a half-peeled banana. Red shirt, a necktie wide enough to serve dinner on. Purple and gold. Boots that—*Boots?* With the trouser legs tucked into the tops of them.

"Sweet Jesus," muttered Heslip. Laughter instead of tension danced in his voice. "No wonder he can only make it with hookers."

They went past on either side, casually, then turned in on him with precision just as he raised his arm to check his watch. Two hard-faced men, one black and broad, the other white and tall, bearing him back against the open door of the booth with their hands stuffed menacingly in the pockets of their dark topcoats.

"She isn't coming," said the white one.

"She's skinny, and a slant besides," said the black one.

"Who . . . what . . ."

"Where's the money?" said the white one.

Sweat stood on Gondolph's face. His eyes darted from one to the other. His skin had gone chalky. "You're . . . police?" he managed to choke out.

"Where's the money?" said the black one.

Gondolph blinked twice and vomited down the front of his suit.

THREE

THE INTERCOM buzzed.

Patrick Michael O'Bannon jerked spasmodically and steaming coffee cascaded down his leg. He yelped.

The intercom buzzed again. O'Bannon regarded it with balefully bloodshot eyes. He set down the half-emptied cup with a slightly tremoring freckled right hand, flexed his fingers, picked up the phone. "O'Bannon," he told the instrument, "go ahead and surprise me."

He listened, his leathery drinker's face sad as a blood-hound's this joyless morning. "Why would Ballard be here?" he asked finally. "Ring *his* extension."

He hung up. He missed. He hung up. From the doorway Ballard's voice said, gently, "That *is* my extension, O'B. You're in my cubicle."

"I . . . what? Oh!"

"Your eyes look like they're bleeding to death."

"You ought to see them from in here. The Great White Father and I closed up the place down on the corner of Franklin last night."

"What kind of shape is *he* in?"

O'B managed to get coffee into his mouth instead of down his leg. "I can't remember." He leaned back carefully in the old swivel chair. With any luck, he'd be dead by noon. "What happened with the embezzler last night?"

Ballard leaned his butt against the edge of the desk. "One look at us, he uppy-chucked all over his necktie."

"Nervous stomach," said O'B sagely.

Despite the booze, he was the best field agent DKA had. He jerked a thumb at the gleaming red length of the Chandra Cadillac which almost blocked the door of the cubicle. The three garage stalls were reserved for hot ones that might get a little ouchy. "That the one you hijacked from me yesterday?"

The intercom buzzed again. This time Ballard picked it up and spoke his name into it. Giselle Marc's voice was full of laughter. "O'B sounds like he's hung over. And la Chandra, your exotic dancer, has arrived to redeem her car. I'm sending her down."

"He is. What's so funny?"

"The look on your face when she gets through with you."

Larry Ballard's face wore an almost savage look of frustration. Chandra, after a full twenty minutes, showed no sign of weakening.

"Why just Chandra?" he broke in with a desperate abruptness. "Why not Miss Chandra or Chandra-something or—"

"Chandra has *style.*"

Looked at dispassionately, Chandra had to be well over sixty. She had an old woman's face and dumpy body. But Ballard had already learned that she was not a person you could look at dispassionately. Maybe he should have run over her when she had darted off the curb in front of the Caddy the day before.

"Style?"

"Chandra is Sanskrit for 'She Outshines the Stars.' Isn't that beautiful?" She nodded to her own question. She had a low-register, almost harsh voice. "Of course it is. Perfect for a dancer. Give me my car."

"I told you several times, Miss—"

"Just Chandra, damn you!"

Ballard gave back a step from the blue eyes blazing in the lined face, even though the top of her gray head came to just above the middle of his chest and showed him pink scalp around the part. Built like a peasant off the steppes of Russia or something, dumpy and shapeless in sweatshirt and Navy peacoat and blue jeans—and what the *hell* was she doing driving a new Cadillac? He tried again.

"Chandra. No money—no car. Savvy? No tickee, no washee. That's it. Final. Over. Done. No more. A lay's a play. You gotta *redeem* it, understand? R-e-d-e-e-m—"

"Give me my car."

He threw up his hands in exasperation, then turned quickly from the obdurate little woman when he heard the glass door of Kearny's cubbyhole in the back of the garage slide open. Thank God, even if the Great White Father *was* nursing a hangover. Chandra was just like talking to the goddam wall, she really was.

Kearny's heavy-jawed face was a bit pale but otherwise he showed no signs of nocturnal carousing with O'Bannon. Ballard walked quickly back to him, the Caddy's distributor rotor safely in his pocket.

"No mention of the five hundred bucks?" asked Kearny.

"Nothing about the comic book, either."

Kearny nodded. He had been studying Chandra as they talked. Odd mixture of age and youth. He knew that what Ballard took for dumpiness was a dancer's thick, muscular body, and that the ankles were thickened with overdeveloped tendons, not age. He moved down the garage.

"Can I help you, ma'am?"

Kearny's basso was hard to argue against, but Chandra tried. "That nasty child refuses to give me back my car."

"Why do you think he took it in the first place?"

"I want my—"

"Two payments delinquent, Chandra—the first two after the down. Another due tomorrow. That's $191.84 each, plus late and repo charges—"

"I'll pay after I have my car back."

Kearny shrugged. "The law gives you five days to redeem. Then the bank has the legal right to resell the vehicle. They will." He turned and started back toward the cubbyhole.

"I'll have this back inside an hour!" she yelled at his back.

Kearny kept going. He slid open the cubbyhole door.

"Philistine!" she yelled.

Kearny disappeared.

Chandra glared after him for a moment, then slid her fierce blue eyes across Ballard as across a dog dropping—was that a hint of laughter in those eyes?—and strode from the garage. Strode, like a man, feet turned out just a bit and heel not really hitting the concrete.

The moment she had disappeared, Kearny came out of his office again. To Ballard's amazement, his face was serious and his cold gray eyes were puzzled.

"It don't wash, Ballard, you follow me? She doesn't know anything about that money, which just ain't reasonable."

The two phone calls came in stacked, like jets in a holding pattern for clearance, almost exactly one hour after Chandra had stalked out. When Giselle Marc buzzed him with the first one, Kearny picked up to find Pete Gilmartin of Golden Gate Trust on the line.

"What gives, Pete?"

"When that Chandra comes back in, release the Caddy to her."

Kearny, stubbing out a cigarette in the overflowing ashtray, paused to say, "She pay you people direct, trying to dodge the repossession charges?"

"Just release it to her, Dan," said Gilmartin in a frustrated voice.

"Now wait a minute—"

"Dammit, d'you think I like it any better than you do?"

Kearny made a wry face and hung up. The moment he did, the intercom buzzed with another call which had been on *Hold.* When he picked up, it was that old friend of all private investigators, the Threatening Phone Call.

"Too bad, Kearny," said the voice.

"Who is this?"

His attention was only half on it, to tell the truth. He was lighting another cigarette and wishing he could quit the damned things.

"Keep looking over your shoulder, Kearny."

Kearny laughed and slammed down the receiver quickly, hoping to catch the caller in the ear with it. Then his face got thoughtful and his eyes hooded. He smoked his cigarette moodily down to where it singed his fingers, hunched forward across the desk as if watching the Late Late Show on a nonexistent television.

Oh, not because of the threat. The locked door and oneway glass of his cubbyhole were to discourage process servers, not assassins. If somebody really *wanted* to get you, he would get you. Kearny's slightly bent and flattened nose, which made him look like an aging club fighter minus cauliflower ears, was a memento from one of the two men who had actually meant it among the literally thousands who had threatened.

No, Kearny was puzzled. Chandra, when she had been in the garage, had not known about the green-backed comic book. Yet an hour later enough pressure had been put on Pete Gilmartin to make him give back the Caddy while it was still delinquent, and a phone call had come from that so-goddam-casual threatening voice they had all picked up from Mafia movies, polished but with the brass showing through. And . . .

Chandra again. Kearny went around the desk and through the door to forestall Ballard. What Ballard didn't know, Ballard couldn't spread around.

"Should I put the rotor back, Mr. Kearny?"

"Do that. And I want some action on that Duster, Larry. I want it today. Cal Cit Bank is boiling."

Ballard cast a glance at Chandra. "It didn't show up at South Park last night, Mr. Kearny."

"Then find out where it is showing up, and drop a rock on it."

"Philistines," said Chandra again, but in a subdued voice.

Kearny waited until Ballard had replaced the rotor and departed, then beamed on the dumpy little woman. "We're ready to release the car to you now, Chandra."

He waited for her to complete the pattern. She did. She said coyly, "You can take what I owe out of the five hundred, can't you?"

The five hundred she hadn't heard of an hour before. He nodded and led her into his office. She sat down in the client's chair across the desk as he checked the file. Two months at $191.84

each, plus late charges of $7.17. For the bank, $390.85. For DKA, repo fee of $47.50, three hours for $37.50 total, eighteen miles for another $4.50 . . .

"Everything in, $480.35," he said. He got the comic book out of the locked middle drawer of one of his filing cabinets.

She sat with the bills from it in her hand, delight dancing in her faded but still somehow young eyes. "All my life I dreamed of a big car of my own," she said softly. "Born in what they called Hell's Kitchen then—Manhattan, Lower West Side. My dad was an immigrant Russian Jew—know what my real name is? Sarah Poplyovin. Can you imagine Sarah Poplyovin dancing for the Crowned Heads?" Her lined face had remarkable animation. "But *Chandra!*"

The light died. She laid the five bills on the desk. Kearny picked them up, riffled them, wrote out a receipt and found a twenty in the wallet he took from his inside suit-jacket pocket.

"You're making sixty-five cents," he told her.

"Thirty. The bus ride. A phone call. Thirty cents you can afford. You have a daughter wants to learn to dance, I'm very good. I'm the best."

She signed the personal property receipt on the condition report. Kearny went out to watch her back the gleaming red monster from the garage, the four sateen pillows under her backside so she could see out. She waved to him, a remarkably graceful flutter of stubby fingers, and went her incongruous way. Kearny mashed the button to lower the heavy steel overhead door. He walked thoughtfully back to his cubbyhole.

One lousy phone call, and the bank would have let her drive that Cadillac out with two payments delinquent and a third coming up tomorrow.

Which meant somebody had a pretty heavy finger on somebody at the bank. Intriguing.

But she had paid, which made it no longer a DKA concern. And, incidentally, defanged the Threatening Phone Call. Their file was *Closed*—or would be as soon as he transferred the money to Golden Gate Trust along with the DKA no-bill statement.

Four

Having left Kearny and the old lady nose-to-nose over the red Caddy, Ballard emerged from the DKA basement into weak noon sunshine and blustery wind. Low clouds which would be fog by nightfall scudded by overhead. One thing you could say for San Francisco, you always had wind. And the rains could start any time.

He drove out toward Howard to find a parking place near Avery Printing. The same fat girl was banging the electric typewriter in the reception area. She had what looked like the same pimples on her chin.

"Gee, you *just* missed Mr. Schilling. By about four minutes."

"Did you give him the business card I left?"

"Um . . . Mr. Avery had that, um . . ."

She stood up suddenly and went to the window. Ballard went with her, wondering what they were supposed to be doing besides not answering his question.

"He left such a little bit ago, I thought maybe we could still see him. Like if he was caught in traffic or something, you know . . ."

The door from the shop area opened and a girl in a long-sleeved velour jersey and Levis staggered out with six boxed reams of paper. Ballard glanced at her, and asked the secretary, "What color is Mr. Schilling's car, do you remember?"

"White."

"Bob Schilling? Was he just here?" The new girl put her load of paper down on the counter beside the front door. She was very good-looking. "I thought he was still in the . . ." She stopped abruptly, looking beyond Ballard at the secretary.

Ballard took his time about glancing back at her himself. "Will you give Mr. Schilling *this* card? It *is* important."

"I'll put it right here beside the typewriter so I don't forget," said the fat girl. She wrote Schilling across the face of the card in big crisp letters.

Ballard nodded and smiled, and winked at the girl in jeans—who was still standing beside her paper with an embarrassed look on her face. Long black hair and light-blue eyes and tawny skin, a really great-looking chick. He glanced back as he started down the stairs: nothing wrong with her backside, either, even in jeans.

That other fat lying bitch, he thought, *just missed him by about four minutes,* then tipping off the good-looking one before she spilled it, *I thought he was still in the*

The what?

Ballard pulled into the big drive-in where South Van Ness and Mission crossed, to order a cheeseburger and coffee. He couldn't stomach that battery acid in the office.

He chewed the hamburger absently as he sorted through assignments, setting up his "swing." An experienced investigator will always arrange the day's work by address, so he doesn't run all over town spinning his wheels instead of working his cases.

still in the

Maybe it *did* help. It told him where Schilling *wasn't.* Nevada, for instance. Or L.A. No place involving a proper name.

still in *the*

Something commonly known, a "the" which was also a place. What place was a . . . what about an institution? A "the" which would keep a guy like Schilling, whose personal life seemed to be going to hell anyway, away from Avery Printing for a recognized, apparently fixed time. Something like thirty days in the county jail, for instance? That would certainly explain why he had dropped so completely out of sight.

He switched on the ignition and the two-way radio came alive, then paid the carhop and called Giselle with his idea.

"I'll get at it, Larry." He could picture the slim blonde in the crowded middle clerical office where the big radio transmitter was: a better investigator than he would ever be, he knew, though she was just his age. She added, "And here's another one: hospitals."

He clipped the mike back on the dash. Jails and hospitals were her work on the phone, not his in the field.

"Because he was turned down by the Air Force," said Bart Heslip to Corinne Jones. "He flunked the physical, so he embezzled seven thou from Fidelity. You explain it, I can't. Over five grand in a paper bag in the Roosevelt Hotel safe, and he acted almost glad we'd caught up with—"

"*Glad?* The man is so scared he throws up on himself, and you say he was *glad?* You terrorized—"

Heslip rolled his eyes heavenward. "Here we go again."

They were having coffee at one of the small high round lacquered tables in the Fatted Calf on Sutter, half a block from the travel agency where Corinne worked. She was a full-bodied woman in a wool knit suit, very chic, her flesh tones a warm café au lait against Heslip's blackness.

"No, honey, we aren't going anywhere again. I know—it's what you do, if it kills you. But I *still* think—"

"I figured you'd be *glad* Dan put me on this kind of case instead of—"

"Which only lasted five days, and—"

Heslip broke out laughing. He drank coffee. "Ain't either of us ever going to finish a sentence."

"What are they going to do to him?"

"Slap his wrist. Fidelity's made a gross recovery of five thou in cash, DKA'll take half of that, so they'll hook Gondolph for another four and a half and come out even."

"That isn't fair! He only took—"

"Lady, he *stole*—not took. They could go for Grand Theft. Instead, they're going to let him get another job and pay them back out of his salary. I'm hoping DKA gets more of this kind of case and that I get to work 'em. The repo end is getting tougher all the time, the way the courts—"

"About time, too," said Corinne in her end-of-discussion voice. Her heart-shaped face, Hamitic in cast rather than Bantu, missed true beauty—if at all—by the narrowest of margins.

Looking at her across the table, Heslip vividly remembered coming out of the coma at Trinity Hospital, after three days in the dark un-world where nothing lived or moved. That face above him, drawn with worry and sleeplessness, those eyes looking down at him with more naked love and pain and delight in them than most men are blessed with in a lifetime.

"But don't let it make you cocky," he said obscurely.

When she looked puzzled, he reached across the table to touch her lips with his fingertip. She was gradually coming to accept the fact that he was a detective, as he had once come to accept the fact he'd never be middleweight champ of the world.

He said mildly, "We're in the age of the deadbeat, baby."

She sighed. "Tomorrow I s'pose you'll be back after them again."

"I s'pose. But chasing Gondolph was *fun.* Know how he blew the two thou he went through? Being bi-i-ig man in a couple of crummy Tenderloin bars. And on hookers. Little and blond and cuddly and with them Dixie vowels." He shook his head. "I can't understand guys that pay for it."

"That's 'cause you don't have to." An utterly bawdy look flashed at him from the comers of her magnificent eyes. "Speaking of that, lover, what time you plan to come over tonight?"

"*There's* an idea!" he exclaimed. "Yeah, man, there's an *idea!*"

"Only if you show up *early.*"

Heslip checked his watch. "I'll beat you home, baby," he promised.

He didn't.

Giselle Marc hung up the phone and leaned back in her swivel chair to massage her temples. She was a tall, lithely built blonde whose aura of wicked sensuality made a lot of men miss the fact that her mental attractions at least equaled her physical ones. Because Kearny hadn't been fooled, she'd been able to develop into a damned good man-hunter. On the wall behind her desk were her three framed licenses: private investigator, repossessor, collector. Not bad for a girl with a master's degree in history from SF State.

So. Hospitals next. No less than eighty-four entries in the San Francisco book, although many of the rest homes and convalescent homes could be eliminated without a call.

The jail idea had been a bust. No record in the county jail down in San Bruno. No record with SFPD or the sheriff's office. Not in the morgue. Negative at the U.S. marshal's office, their contact at the FBI, the . . .

The phone rang.

Giselle sighed. It was 5:20; from the line it was coming in on, probably a client with a bitch. Most client complaints eventually filtered through to her.

"Oh! Hi, Pete!" she exclaimed. Unconsciously she leaned closer to the phone. She liked Pete Gilmartin, liked him a lot. Then she said "Oh!" again, and "Don't tell me we've got more grief on that Chandra car."

"Can't I just be calling my favorite private eye to say hello?"

"It would be the first time."

He laughed. "Matter of fact, I *am* calling about the Chandra file. The high mucky-mucks liked DKA's work on it so much that they told me to hand more assignments to you people. Can the Great Dan K come up here in person to pick them up?"

"Anything for you, Petie-boy."

"*Any*thing?"

"In a business way."

Gilmartin sighed gustily, then said "Huh?" to someone beside his desk. He came back to Giselle. "Tell the Great White Father to be here by five forty-five sharp, or we'll give 'em to the competition."

She had just delivered the message to Kearny, who'd come up for a cup of coffee from the dark little kitchen behind Giselle's office, when the radio said: "SF-7 calling San Francisco KDM 366."

"This is KDM 366, go ahead."

Giselle left "Control" off because SF-7, a new man named Dunford who'd come highly recommended from an agency in Seattle, had put "San Francisco" in front of the call letters. It was an alerting signal. She was aware of Kearny at her elbow, stirring his instant coffee.

"Is Mr. Bush of the bank's legal department there?"

Kearny took the mike. "This is Bush. What's the problem?"

"Are you familiar with the Norman Twiggs file, sir?"

"I certainly am."

Giselle was already flicking through the CAL CIT *Open* tub beside her desk, to flop the TWIGGS file under Kearny's nose. Dunford had explained to Mr. Twiggs that the radio had a direct tie-in to California Citizens Bank, and he wanted Mr. Bush to talk to Mr. Twiggs, since Mr. Twiggs wouldn't surrender his car. It was a drill Kearny had worked out to help cool potentially explosive situations where the field agent felt he was in trouble.

"Mr. Twiggs, I have to say frankly that I don't understand your attitude . . ." Kearny went on at length, his eyes roaming the unfamiliar file for facts to support the idea that he was intimately acquainted with the subject's delinquent contract. ". . . signed with you in good faith, Mr. Twiggs, and you have reacted with a threat of force to the bank's legal representative . . ."

Kearny released the *Transmit* button to let Twiggs stammer hesitantly into the unfamiliar microphone. He turned to Giselle. "Better call Ed Dorsey on the intercom; tell him to get up to the bank for me. He can use my station wagon. The keys are over the visor."

It was 5:31 P.M.

At 5:34 Bart Heslip parked in front of the primary school across from DKA. That side of the street was tow-away in the mornings but not the afternoons. Ed Dorsey came from the DKA basement and turned toward Franklin. Heslip locked the Plymouth, thinking that Kearny ought to transfer that old fart into inside skip-tracing, where he could do all his work on the phone. He wasn't worth a damn on the street.

The lights came on as Heslip crossed toward the curb where a few months before he had been struck down with a blackjack. Three days of coma. He unconsciously fingered the tiny scar at the base of his throat where the tracheal tube had been.

He reached the curb. Two bulky men walking briskly up from Franklin had just come abreast of Dorsey, who was opening the door of Kearny's station wagon. One of the men hit Dorsey in the face. Heslip saw the glint of the horn-rim glasses flying off. Dorsey went over backward into the cyclone fence that separated the sidewalk from the blacktop parking lot flanking it. He screamed. The scream seemed to cut Bart Heslip off at the knees. The second man drove a fist into Dorsey's stomach.

Concussion. Three days in coma.

The first man slammed Dorsey face-first into the fence. It made a *spronging* sound against his face.

No metal plate in Heslip's head, but almost.

Fists were thudding into Ed Dorsey's kidneys.

One more blow, Dr. Arnold Whitaker had said. One more traumatic shock to Heslip's skull, and it would have been . . .

Dorsey was down on his hands and knees where a heavy shoe could snap his head back. A haze of bloody spray flew up off his face, as if he were a fighter taking an uppercut under the lights. His upper plate arced into the gutter like a fighter's dislodged mouthpiece.

And Heslip was suddenly a fighter again, not a man afraid another concussion would turn him into vegetable soup. Nine seconds had passed. He dropped his attaché case and charged.

The stompers looked up, startled. They ran. Heslip was smaller, faster, in superb shape as always. The first reached their car, parked at the corner with the motor running for a quick left uphill into Franklin no matter what the three-way traffic light said. The second shot a quick look back and ran into a parking meter. It spun him halfway around, so that a rock-hard left hook could smash into his short ribs.

"Gugnh!" he said in response to the hook.

It was his only comment for a number of hours, because he was hit eight times in the face before he could fall down. As the stolen car spun into Franklin and was gone, the man it had abandoned received a broken nose, a detached retina in the left eye, and lost three teeth. He swallowed a fourth tooth and got a hairline jaw fracture when his chin hit the pavement.

Dan Kearny dragged away the black detective, who was still clubbing vicious lefts and rights, a few moments later. Up in the deserted clerical offices, Giselle Marc was already phoning for an ambulance.

FIVE

LINCOLN WAY parallels Golden Gate Park from Arguello all the way to the ocean, serving as one edge of the area San Franciscans call the Sunset. On relatively few days, however, does Lincoln Way see the sun before noon, and on many days, loses it by four. When Ballard pulled aside the second-hand lace curtains of his bulbous living-room window, there was only a gray wall of fog instead of the broad cheerful green stretches of Golden Gate Park.

At 8:07 in the goddam morning.

He returned to the Salvation Army easy chair, which was the room's main item of furniture, to sip from the cup of scalding coffee balanced on the arm. Coffee was almost the only thing culinary, apart from hamburgers, that Ballard did. He did it superbly. His coffee could have won prizes.

His reports were up to date; if he went in now, Kearny would come up with some shit detail for him to do. A flooring check. Return a car to a dealer. Shop some hunk of tin from the Florida Street storage lot for bids—after first starting it with jumper cables because the battery would be dead. Better skip-tracing at home.

He consulted the Yellow Pages open to HOSPITALS in his lap, then started dialing the phone. Seven hospitals later a female voice from Records said, "Yes, we have a Schilling, Robert."

Ballard slammed an exultant fist into the chair arm. His half-full coffee cup fell off the other arm into the waste-basket. He left it there. He wanted that Duster.

Kaiser Hospital is set back from and above Geary Boulevard, giving patients whose rooms chance to face that way some nice views of the city. Ballard went in the Emergency entrance to thread his way to the front lobby, where a Visitor's Aid lady smiled in false-toothed gentility from behind a table.

"Mr. Schilling is in room . . . ten-thirty. The elevators . . ."

Ballard had seen that one of the potted plants on her table had *Bob Schilling* written in a slanting feminine hand on its white envelope.

"That looks like it needs water. I could take it up—"

"How nice," ticked the false teeth. "Please follow the yellow line on the tenth floor."

Ballard and an elderly white couple shared the elevator with a young hip black orderly spaced out on dope or the euphoria of living.

"Hair between my toes, man," he said to them. The elevator was inching along with the speed of a house being jacked up. "This elevator so slow I grow hair between my toes ridin' it."

"Does it tickle?"

His face contorted in a wheezy paroxysm of laughter. He slapped his thigh. "*Neet!*" he cried. "Jes' spray it on an' *smoo-o-oth* hair away!"

The elderly couple had punched nine when they had gotten on. They crowded off hastily at four. Ballard, at ten, began following the yellow line on the floor like Dorothy following the yellow-brick road. It took him around several comers and down hallways and along a glassed-in balcony overlooking a court. From this he edged through a sliding-glass door into room 1030.

Two of the beds held very old and approximately dead-looking patients. The one in the middle was occupied by a man in his mid-thirties who had thinning black hair awry across the forehead of a pale, sharp-featured face.

Ballard raised the droopy plant for inspection. "From the gang down at Avery Printing. It needs water."

"Hey, that's nice of them."

He handed the card to Schilling and took the plant into the bathroom to run water into it at the sink. Bingo! It was the right Bob Schilling.

He emerged to find Schilling sitting up straighter against his mound of pillows with a sharp look on his face. "This ain't from Avery Printing."

"Where's the Duster, Bob?"

The old man closest to the hall door, who had something dripping into him from a bottle suspended beside the bed, croaked, "How can a man sleep with everybody talking?"

"Shit, you sleep twenty hours a day the way it is," said Schilling.

"I'll ring for the nurse if you don't stop your obscenities."

"Shitshitshitshitshitshit. How's that, you old bastard?"

The decrepit oldster on the other side began to moan.

"Where's the Duster?" asked Ballard.

"Screw you. My name isn't on the contract."

"You'll end up paying for it. Joanne will see to that."

"Noisy bastards," exclaimed the old man who didn't like swearing.

The other old man quit groaning abruptly. He opened a pair of very blue eyes to regard Ballard with calm deliberation. He winked. He closed his eyes. He started to groan again.

"What's his problem?" Ballard asked.

"I'd know?"

"What's yours?"

"Hernia operation," said Schilling.

Ballard grinned. "Strained a gut on her, huh?"

Schilling's already pale face turned to skim milk. Good. Get him sore enough, he might spill something useful. Or strain another gut.

Then the humor of it struck Schilling too. He suddenly grinned. Ballard suddenly liked him.

"Christ, man, don't make me laugh! Laughing and coughing . . . Say, if I give up the Duster, will Joanne get it back?"

"Only if she pays the three delinquent payments and the late charges and all of the charges we've run up looking for it."

Schilling relaxed against the pillows again. "Yeah. Okay. Me and Emma's heading south, anyway, man. South of the border. Duster's at the far end of St. Joe's, where it deadends at Turk. The keys are under the floor mat on the driver's side."

"Thanks." Ballard paused at the sliding door to the glassed-in balcony. "I hope Joanne doesn't catch up with you."

"No way. We'll be long gone in two more days. I was hero of the floor this morning, man. Had the ward nurse and the doctor and the orderlies and the nurse's aid in here just about applauding—"

"How come?"

"I took a piss." Then he started to laugh. Very carefully.

That lying bitch at Avery Printing. White, she had said. The Duster was two-toned blue filmed with street dust from being parked a mere two blocks from the hospital for several days. Ballard found the keys and fired it up and pulled it out of the slot so he could drop his company car in.

The Duster went into the storage lot under the freeway; after Ballard had made out the condition report, he went into the DKA basement to phone the repossession in to the police in case Schilling should change his mind and report it stolen. It had happened before, often. Then he went upstairs to Clerical to report the repossession once again. Legal notices had to be sent, the client notified, the police report confirmed in writing.

As he came into the front office that stared down at Golden Gate through narrow, grimy bay windows, Jane Goldson raised a pert face from her typing. "It's you, is it? They've been going mad all morning trying to reach you."

Ballard searched uneasily through his mind for whatever it was he must have screwed up. He pulled assignments from his *In* box with a feigned nonchalance. "I was home until after nine. If you wanted me . . ."

"I tried. I couldn't get through. Calling all your birds, one after another?"

Jane was a devastating English girl, slim and vibrant, with exciting chestnut hair two-thirds of the way down her back and exciting miniskirts two-thirds of the way up her thighs. It was the bane of Ballard's existence that she refused to mess around with anyone from DKA.

"I was skip-tracing. In fact"—he leaned forward to drop the condition report on her desk—"the Schilling Duster's in the barn."

"Got that, did you? That's a good one, I'll call Cal Cit so they can do their little bird over it."

"Ah . . . you don't know what Kearny wanted me for, do you?"

Her face sobered abruptly. "Oh, that's terrible, you can't have heard! Ed Dorsey was horribly beat up last night."

Six

"Four busted ribs, ruptured spleen—these ain't in the order of importance, Dan. Skull fracture. One finger so badly crushed they still might have to take it off. Jaw broken in three places. Bruised kidneys. Dislocated left knee. Multiple cuts, bruises and lacerations." Benny Nicoletti had been speaking in a surprisingly high, soft voice for someone weighing over two-twenty. "And he's sixty-two years old."

"None of that explains why you're here, Benny," said the detective patiently. "A cop comes around, sure. General Works—maybe. But from the Police Intelligence Unit? No way."

"Thing is, we got a make on Garofolo that your boy Heslip took to pieces." He shook his head. "When somebody, even somebody like Bart, can do that to a professional—"

"Professional?" demanded Kearny sharply.

"Semi-pro. Minor enforcer, got a rap sheet back East going back to when he got out of the Army in 1947. Seven arrests, all strong-arm—assault or ADW. Brought to trial three times, never took a fall. Nol-prossed once, two dismissed for lack of evidence."

"Clean in California?"

"Until now. Works as a checker on the loading docks for an outfit over in Walnut Creek called Padilla Trucking." He paused. "Makes you sort of wonder what a cat like that would have against old Ed Dorsey."

"Why don't you ask him?"

"Right now he ain't able to talk. They'll arraign him as soon as he can stand up, then we'll see."

He leaned forward and his voice suddenly hardened. "Come on, Dan, what are you guys into that gets a systematic beating assigned to one of your men?"

"Nothing, not a damn thing." *Assigned* beating. That explained Benny Nicoletti of Police Intelligence showing up: the rackets was one of his jobs. But it didn't explain the beating itself. Kearny smiled sardonically. "I thought there wasn't any organized crime in San Francisco, Benny."

Nicoletti, suddenly agitated, stood up and began pacing back and forth in front of Kearny's desk. On his feet he was a startlingly big man who prowled rather than walked; he could have been a pro linebacker except for being in his mid-forties. His high-pitched voice was thick and bitter.

"Say you got a little bookie business that starts getting trade away from the old established firms, Dan. Pretty soon a guy gets off a jet from New York or Detroit and comes into your shop and sets his suitcase on the counter. He opens up the suitcase and lets you look at what's inside, and says 'Don't do it no more' and shuts up the suitcase and catches the next jet back to New York or Detroit. But there ain't no organized crime in this city, hell no."

"Just a bunch of gifted amateurs," said Kearny.

Nicoletti stopped pacing. He put his knuckles on the desk to lean across it. "I hate those bastards' guts. All of 'em."

Kearny, still seated, nodded at him across the desk. "I'll let you know if anything turns up."

"Yeah, I bet you will," said Nicoletti in bitter disbelief. At the door, he paused with his hand on the latch to look back. "Another thing I hate, Kearny, is crooked cops who spend their time spotting hot cars for some private outfit rather than for the city what's paying them a salary. I'd just love for us to fall on somebody in the department one of these days and find out he's got a hand in your pocket."

Kearny leaned back in his swivel chair. He very deliberately cocked his feet on top of the desk. "How long've I known you, Benny?" he asked. "Fifteen years?"

"About that," admitted Nicoletti.

"I ever wave a dollar bill at you?"

"You know you ain't. But that don't mean—"

"How many years did your daughter work for us, summers, typing skip letters, Benny? How many cars you bought from us? Where'd your kid get the great deal on that big old Harley he rides?"

Nicoletti's round, mild face had darkened as Kearny talked. Now two spots of pink burned on his cheeks. He slid open the door and went out through it and slid it shut behind him without any sound except that of the door sliding on the runners. He didn't look back.

Kearny leaned forward to stub out his cigarette. He lit another. He sat quietly, frowning. He had to have room to move around in, now that the fact Police Intelligence was interested had made it sure. Benny'd get over it a lot sooner than old Ed Dorsey was going to get over having his face walked on.

He mashed Giselle's intercom button. "Quit using Waterreus. For anything, anything at all. Got that?"

"Sure, Dan'l, but he's the only cop on the payroll. Who's going to turn hot cars for us off the skip list if—"

"You, O'B, Kathy, Bart and Larry for a meeting in the front clerical office at six o'clock," said Kearny, ignoring her remark about Waterreus. "Everybody else out. *Everybody.*"

Whoever it was had screwed up badly in letting his errand boy get picked off by Bart Heslip. Because now DKA was going to start finding out who. And why.

Golden Gate Trust was a three-year-old independent bank. Because it was so new, and small, it had been aggressive in getting clients, and from the beginning, had specialized in automotive financing. In an age when many dealers carried their own paper, this meant more than competitive interest rates, kicking back part of the interest to the dealer so he could sell at a narrower margin, far from stringent flooring policies, and accepting a greater percentage of marginal risks on auto loans.

All of which, in turn, meant that Golden Gate Trust got burned more often than other banks, and thus needed investigation, skip-tracing and repossession services more often, too.

Auto Loans occupied a full third of the ground floor, running down the right side of the building. The rest was taken up with normal banking functions, tellers' windows, bank officers. Kearny found Pete Gilmartin at his small glassed-in office to the rear.

He started up from behind his desk when Kearny appeared. "Jesus, Dan, what say?" They shook hands. "You guys must be in fat city down there at DKA."

"Why do you say that, Pete?"

"I expected you to come panting up here last night by five forty-five to pick up all those new assignments—"

"You didn't hear? Kathy didn't call and tell you?" Kearny asked it with every indication of astonishment, although he had given Kathy strict orders not to. "I got jammed up on the radio, three guys trying to fit a set of tire chains to one of my men, so I sent Ed Dorsey . . ."

Gilmartin listened open-mouthed, a curly-haired man in his late twenties with sideburns which almost but not quite ruptured bank decorum. Gilmartin's suit hovered on the same fine edge. Kearny admired it as a remarkable performance of being a company man with flair.

". . . anyway, Pete, I hope you didn't dish all the cases out to the competition as a result . . ."

Gilmartin was grinning. He had a wide engaging smile, dimples and a cleft chin. A young man to be AVP; he'd make VP within three years, Kearny figured.

"The man upstairs specified you people, Dan. I just said that to Giselle because I love to hear her plead the cause of old DK and A."

For the next ten minutes they went through the sheaf of square yellow referral cards he had taken from his bottom desk drawer.

Kearny finally folded and pocketed them. "Which VP gets an extra case of booze at Christmas for this, Pete?" he asked casually.

"That's a funny one, Dan, now you mention it. Art Nucci in Personal Loans. I didn't think, between you and me, he could even *read* an auto contract, let alone—"

"You know how they rotate these veeps, Pete. He'll probably be down here taking on-the-job training with you next week."

Outside, Kearny lit a cigarette before getting into the wagon he had left parked in the yellow zone on Austin Alley.

Art Nucci, Vice-President in Charge of Personal Loans. Unless Gilmartin was lying, of course.

Seven

Giselle Marc paused with the coffeepot in the narrow doorway of the front office, thinking to herself that there was a lot of diverse human talent, oddly channeled, in that room.

Over by the doorway to Kathy's office, Kathy and Bart Heslip had their heads together. Almost surely telling dirty jokes; neither ever told them to anyone else.

Behind Jane Goldson's desk sat Larry Ballard, good-looking in a windblown, outdoorsy way—despite the fact that the closest he ever willfully got to the rural scene was abalone-diving up the coast on free weekends.

O'Bannon, slumped in his chair with his topcoat still on, studying the new assignments he'd just collected from his *In* box. Three drinks ahead of everybody else, of course. Started as a collector for a jewelry firm when he'd gotten out of the Navy, had gone with Walter's Auto Detectives in 1955 and, like Kathy, left for the formation of DKA in 1964. Chronically drinking too much, just coasting along on experience these days—but still the best man they had when he bore down.

"Who wants coffee?"

Ballard saw the pot in her hand. "You mean that's *brewed* coffee?"

"Specially for you, Larry."

And what about Giselle Marc, she thought as she poured and passed Pream and sugar. Twenty-six, the same age as Ballard but with five more years in the game than him. Started out typing skip letters for the just-formed DKA at eighteen, working after school and summers until she'd gotten her B.A. and M.A. in history from SF State, then coming to work full time.

What compulsion did she share with the others that kept her here instead of teaching, as she once had so confidently expected to do?

Frankly, who gave a damn? She loved it, and she was good at it.

The stairwell door slammed. Kearny's heavy footsteps came up the uncarpeted wooden stairs. He entered the crowded office stripping off his topcoat.

"We're all fired?" suggested O'Bannon.

"Try to ram another expense account like that last one down my throat, O'B, and you might be." He looked over at Kathy. "What's the latest word on Ed Dorsey?"

"Still critical, but they have hopes."

"Anybody been to see him yet?"

Giselle cut in: "His wife won't let us, Dan. She told the hospital no visitors from DKA, none at all."

"Beautiful," snorted Kearny.

Same old crap, DKA getting blamed for the garbage, as if they dumped it instead of poking through it. He sat down on the edge of the desk opposite the hall doorway so he could see them all. He nodded his heavy graying head. "You all know what happened to Ed last night. The police don't like it, but because they can't prove anything they'll have to go along with the theory that he was attacked by mistake. We want them to keep thinking that for a while."

"You're saying it wasn't just a mugging?" demanded Heslip in a surprised voice.

"It was a setup; I was supposed to come out of the office between five-thirty and five-forty and get into the station wagon. They hit Ed as soon as he opened my car door because they thought he was me."

From the corner of his eye he saw Giselle open her mouth as the implications sank in, but he went right on without giving her a chance to speak. "We have four places to dig at the moment. Chandra. The AVP in charge of Auto Contracts at Golden Gate Trust, Pete Gilmartin. The VP in charge of Personal Loans, also at GG Trust, Arthur Nucci. And an East Bay drayage firm called Padilla Trucking."

"Can you sort of explain who and why?" asked Kathy Onoda.

"Larry walked in between Chandra and a payoff man with a fistful of hundred-dollar bills. She didn't know about the bills when she came to redeem, stormed out vowing to have the car back inside an hour. An hour later I got two phone calls. Golden Gate Trust told me to give the car back to her, paid-up or not. The other told me to keep looking over my shoulder. Then Chandra came back knowing all about the money, and mentioned in passing that she'd made a phone call."

"To whoever pressured the bank and threatened you, obviously," said O'Bannon. "But why the strong-arm stuff after you'd already given her the car back?"

"That's one of the things we have to find out."

O'B briskly nodded his gleaming red head. "How do you want to split up the work, Dan?"

"You and Kathy are out of it. But you'll have to cover for the others, so I wanted—"

"What the hell?" O'B demanded angrily.

"Married," said Kearny. "Both of you."

Everyone paused to think that one over. Kathy broke it first, with a high tinkling laugh like the formalized giggling of geisha girls in Japanese movies. It was nothing at all like her southern-slut laugh.

"When did *you* get so cautious, Dan?"

"Benny Nicoletti of Police Intelligence was around. He told me without telling me, if you get what I mean, that the boy Bart laid down—Garofolo—is a syndicate enforcer. Long pedigree back East, lots of arrests and no convictions. I don't want anyone on the case who's vulnerable because of family."

He said nothing of the fact that he was married, with three kids. It was an inescapable hazard: Kearny *was* DKA.

"What about Corinne?" asked Heslip.

"After tonight, contact her by phone only. Don't go near her."

"*Whooie!*" he exclaimed in his detachable accent. "That high-yaller gonna take this chile's head right *off* she hears 'bout dis hyar dang'r'us 'ssignment."

"Tell her Dan has *you* down in L.A. doing a flooring check on a warehouse full of color TVs," Kathy said callously.

"Ah, so, you ver' smart Japonee girr."

"Now lissen hyar, Kingfish . . ."

"The floor show over?" demanded Kearny.

They subsided abruptly.

Ballard had been listening rather than talking. This was really going to be something! *Really* doing detective work, really digging. The first case he had really dug on had been a gypsy fortune-teller. That was when he'd realized he was a detective.

"Where's the tie-in with this East Bay trucking firm?" he asked.

"Bart's boyfriend works for them. Garofolo."

"*Worked.*" Heslip laughed suddenly. "When I hits 'em, man, they stays hit!"

Ballard made a rude noise. Kearny asked if there were any questions. No questions. No requests for handgun permits; these people were professionals who knew you only wanted a gun when you were completely sure you'd be willing to use it.

"I've got a spaghetti feed laid on at Rocca's," said Kearny. He added to O'B, "With lots of dago red." As they began reaching for their coats, he stopped them once again. "All of you keep a sharp eye on your own back trail. If you cut someone else's tracks, let me know right away. *Right* away."

Giselle walked the two blocks to Rocca's with Kearny. "You don't *really* think Pete set you up, do you, Dan?"

Kearny shrugged. "Him or Nucci—or somebody in between, like a secretary."

"I can't believe Pete . . ." She stopped. If Gilmartin hadn't been married, with a couple of kids, she might . . . "Do you know exactly what it is we're trying to find?"

"Connections. Anything that sticks out, doesn't fit, doesn't make sense."

"Like a sixty-year-old dancer, who can barely pay her studio rent, driving a ten-thousand-dollar car?"

"Exactly like that," said Kearny.

EIGHT

THERE IS nothing glamorous about asking questions, but it is what detectives do. Hundreds of questions, of dozens of individuals, firms, groups. Personal questions. Business questions. Social questions. Asked in person in the field, asked by phone from the office.

Asking questions means long hours, because you have to talk to people when they are available, not when you are. It means role-playing, because many people won't talk to investigators. Not glamorous—but because of the endless variables in the human equation, seldom dull.

Kearny had his meeting on a Friday night. On Saturday morning they sorted out assignments. By midweek, he knew, information would be piling up.

Padilla Trucking.

Because there was a good chance Garofolo's unknown partner might also work for the trucking firm, it was Larry Ballard instead of Bart Heslip who showed up in Walnut Creek on Monday morning looking for work. Unsuccessfully.

"Padilla Trucking doesn't hire drivers," he explained on Tuesday morning to Kearny. "You have to own your truck-trailer rig, and you sign with Padilla as an independent contractor."

Kearny ran a thoughtful hand through his graying hair, worn a trifle longer than the year before. "*Own* your truck—or lease it?"

"Oh! That's right. Lease it—and only from Padilla. But hell, Dan, the understanding is that your payments are going toward your purchase of the rig. According to the general manager, a guy named DeSimone, you make so much bread that you own the rig within about three years . . ."

"Let me tell you how I think it works, Giselle," said Kearny later. He was leaning against the edge of the rangy blonde's desk, slurping too-hot instant coffee. "Padilla Trucking gets a lot of business because they bid lower on jobs than any legitimate trucking outfit can—which they can do because of two factors. First, they gimmick their scales so they overload their trucks. If a driver gets busted by the state for overloading—what the hell, he's an independent contractor, you follow me? Second, they pay their drivers substandard rates, because the poor bastards have signed a lease contract agreement which stipulates they'll take whatever jobs Padilla offers them—at Padilla's rates."

"But in three years, when the driver gets his truck paid off . . ."

"Not in three years, not ever. Padilla makes sure that eventually he starts falling behind in his payments. Then the agreement is declared in default, and the truck-trailer is repossessed. The driver finds the payments he thought were going into equity really have been eaten up by interest and carrying charges. And then Padilla leases it all over again to another driver."

Giselle shook her head. "It sure *sounds* like a Mafia operation."

"It is. Benny coming around confirms that." He stood up with a wry face. "Jesus, that's lousy coffee. Our problem is whether Garofolo and his partner were on syndicate business when they jumped Ed, or were doing a little moonlighting on the side. I hoped Larry could get in over there to find out, but . . ."

Giselle's blue eyes suddenly challenged him across the desk. "How about my checking with the state to find out who the stockholders in the Padilla corporation are? If we can establish a connection between one of them and Nucci at Golden Gate Trust . . ."

Kearny noted that she excluded any possibility that Pete Gilmartin might be involved. He nodded. "Let me know when you have something, Giselle."

Peter Gilmartin.

Heslip found that Gilmartin had a tract house in Edgemar, in the San Mateo County fog belt three or four miles south of the county line. A great view of the Pacific sparkling to the west—when the fog let you see it. Three-bedroom, two-bath on a standard lot, frame-and-stucco California bungalow.

"Twenty-nine thousand with a twenty-year mortgage," he told Giselle. He'd run the lot number through the San Mateo County courthouse in Redwood City to get ownership data. "Two-car garage, but one side full of the kids' toys and camping gear. Neighbors confirm: one car, a two-year-old Chevy wagon."

Giselle copied down the license. "I'll run it through DMV, find out whether they have any other vehicles and who holds the pink on the wagon. We can get a copy of his credit app and the name of his insurance broker from the financing institution . . ." She paused. "He looks pretty clean so far, doesn't he, Bart?"

"Yeah. Kids in the Little League; he pitches softball for the bank-sponsored team. His wife belongs to a bowling team from the dry-cleaning shop where she used to work before they got married. Hell of a good-looking woman." He scratched the back of his neck thoughtfully. "Be interesting, of course, if he owned that Chevy outright. AVP can't make more than a grand a month . . ."

Giselle sighed. "I'd better try to bluff the phone company out of his long-distance phone records for the past few months, too."

Arthur Nucci.

Ballard and Heslip together had begun looking Nucci over on Sunday. He was going to be a thornier problem than Gilmartin, because a man making fifty to sixty grand a year can—given an inheritance or a break in the market—legitimately account for quite a bit of excess cash.

"*Whoee!*" exclaimed Heslip. "I figure this mother's going to *need* an explanation."

Ballard shook his head. "What do you figure he pays in taxes?"

Nucci lived in a house the grounds of which covered a quarter of a block in the exclusive St. Francis Woods area. Two-story pseudo-Mission pseudo-adobe, with the red-tiled roof so popular with this sort of 1930s California construction. A sparkling black Fleetwood ran puddles of water onto the broad concrete apron in front of the garage.

"The last time I worked anything in St. Francis Woods was the Mayfield case," said Ballard.

"A long time ago, man." A black chauffeur had come from the garage to begin wiping down the Fleetwood with a damp chamois cloth. "Hang loose, I got an idea."

Ballard kept walking. He heard Heslip's cheery "What say, brother?" before he was out of earshot. The Fleetwood had PS plates, so it was a bank car. Ten minutes later Heslip joined him to display a five-dollar bill. He was laughing so hard he almost fell down.

"Told him I was collectin' from the brothers for the Black Panther's breakfast program, and damned if he didn't shell out! Looked scared shitless." His eyes gleamed sardonically in his black face. "He sure hates Nucci's guts. Three servants—him, a white cook-housekeeper he says is new, a white yardman who comes in twice a week."

"Anything interesting?"

"Mercedes in the garage, and Jeter—that's the chauffeur—says Nucci and his wife drove the Chrysler wagon up to their weekend place by Lake Tahoe. South Shore, he says."

Two cars, that house, summer home . . . A lot of bread. Ballard swung the Plymouth over to Portola, took it through the aimless clots of Sunday traffic.

"Wish I could have got the address of the summer place, but I couldn't think of a way a Panther could have asked."

"Machine-gunned the garage first?" Ballard pulled abruptly off into a shopping area. "I got an idea, Bart."

They went over to the pay phone.

"Mr. Arthur Nucci, please, California Highway Patrol calling." He listened. "I see. Can you tell me where to get in touch with him, ma'am? We have reason to believe he might have witnessed a hit-run accident on California Fifty near Echo Summit yesterday and . . . No, ma'am, he's not in trouble. But he may have witnessed . . ."

He hung up and scribbled down the address.

"In a district called Skyland," he told Heslip. "Apparently it's a few miles out of South Lake Tahoe." He did a creditable imitation of a woman's voice, "Bill Harrah has a place out there!"

"Ole Marse Nucci do seem to do well by hisse'f, don't he?"

"Yeah. What say we drive up to Tahoe—"

"Better cool that, man. Tomorrow morning bright and early you've got to go out to Padilla Trucking and be a truck driver."

Which, of course, had resulted in Ballard's learning that Padilla Trucking had no employee-drivers. Only yardmen who fractured old detectives' skulls.

NINE

CHANDRA.

Since the old dancer was the focal point of the whole problem, whatever that problem was going to be, Kearny took her himself. Besides, he wanted to get to hell out of the office on that Monday morning.

Before leaving, he called the sales manager of Curtiss Cadillac, in an old ornate building left over from the days when Van Ness Avenue had proudly called itself Auto Row.

"Lou? Dan Kearny here. Who do you like at Candlestick on Sunday?"

"Forty-niners."

"You've got ten bucks at six-to-four, okay?" Before Cassavette could respond, he asked, "What can you tell me about a Chandra, that's C-h-a-n-d-r-a, no first name, no initial, who bought a new convertible a couple of months back?"

"Old gray-haired broad runs a dance studio?" he asked, obviously around his cigar.

"That's the one. She make the down by cash or check?"

"Second. I'll look." Cassavette had recently switched to Curtiss from Crescent Lincoln-Mercury; Kearny wasn't sure he'd made the right move. He came back. "Check. We wouldn't give her delivery until it cleared . . ."

"Bad credit?"

"*No* credit. Rent, phone, utilities—what the hell's that?"

"Yeah, what bank?"

Cassavette told him, adding that it was the North Beach branch at Columbus and Green. "Somebody got miseries on her now?"

"Naw. She pimpled a parked car up in Pacific Heights, insurance company is trying to deal because the car she hit was supposed to be garaged in Marin where the rates are lower."

Ten minutes later he parked the wagon at the top of the hill in front of Mike's Grocery. Chandra's studio was a short half-block away, where Edith Alley cut off the odd-number, downhill side of Grant. Just beyond, Grant itself swooped down toward the Embarcadero. Kearny had once questioned a girl in a flat on Edith. He grinned at the memory. It had been one of Ballard's first cases, and he'd wanted to paste Kearny in the mouth for making the sweet young thing cry.

Chandra's studio was in a three-story apartment house which had been built when bays were still in but Victorian curlicues were out. The frame building had been battleship-gray in some distant past, with white trim; now it was peeling to show the wood beneath. The big front window and narrow yellow door of the studio faced directly on the sidewalk. The glass in each had been painted over on the inside. CHANDRA arced across the window in foot-high amateur lettering, with *the dance* in yellow script beneath. No hours were shown.

The yellow door was locked. Above it were screwed the metal numbers 1719, painted a smeary red, next to a painted-over but still visible LIPTON'S TEA. Old grocery store? Mike on the corner would probably know.

The bright-eyed, burly merchant was talking in rapid-fire Italian with an old woman dressed in black. Kearny bought an Eskimo Pie.

"What time's the dance studio open up?"

"Chandra's?" Mike laid a thick hairy hand on the minute counter behind which he passed his days, leaned forward as if to look down toward the studio. He gave a heavy laugh. "Whenever she feels like it. That old girl ain't afraid of work—she'll lay down alongside it any time."

"She had the place long?"

"Six years, maybe. I used to have a grocery store in there."

Kearny got the name and address of the building owner. Leaving, he drove by 574 Greenwich, half a block away, where Chandra lived. A single-unit dwelling, fairly rare on Telegraph Hill, built back from and well above the steeply slanting street. The gray-concrete retaining wall was flush with the sidewalk, twenty feet high on the uphill side, thirty on the downhill, crumbling in places to show rusted reinforcing rod.

Kearny stared at it through the open window and drummed thoughtful fingers on the steering wheel. Going up between hunched concrete shoulders was a set of steep narrow stairs. These ended in a narrow walk to the front door through the vast profusion of waist-high bushes and shrubs which covered the sloping yard. Foliage dripped down over the lip of the retaining wall like melted wax from a candle.

Where could the original point of contact possibly be between *this*—Chandra—and a heavy who would hire a beating and pressure a banker at a mere phone call? More important, who was he? Talking some facts about Chandra's finances out of her bank might help . . .

Friday again. Kearny was explaining to the others why he had taken a chance and posed as a state banking commission investigator to Chandra's bank, rather than getting information through channels.

"Sure, DKA does work for their head office, but bankers tend to drink from the same bottle. Word might have filtered back to whoever is involved at Golden Gate Trust. This way, the branch people are playing industrial spy and keeping their mouths shut."

"It's still a felony if you get caught," Ballard pointed out.

"Misdemeanor in this state. Okay: Chandra has lived at 574 Greenwich since 1938. The old Italian landlord charges her a hundred a month and could be getting two-fifty, but she *still* has trouble making the rent. Chinese landlord of the dance studio has threatened eviction for non-payment twice in the six years she's been there. She grosses between five and six bills a month from the studio; no other apparent sources of income."

"And driving a new Cadillac," said Heslip. "That's beautiful."

"It gets better. On July thirtieth she deposited five thousand dollars in cash in her checking account, bringing the balance to $5,027.38. Between then and August eleventh, checks totaling $1,994.12 passed through the account, written to Grant Avenue and Union Street boutiques, and a sizable one to an athletic-supply house for new exercise bars for the studio. On August eleventh she wrote a check to Curtiss Cadillac for $3,094.45 to cover down, tax and license on the Caddy. She got a good deal because it was the end of the model year."

"She also got overdrawn," said Giselle.

"Would have if she hadn't made her regular deposit from the dance-studio receipts. As it was, the check cleared. No further large deposits, but last week she used five one-hundred-dollar bills to pay off the auto delinquency. Reactions?"

"Blackmail," said Giselle and Heslip together. Heslip went on, "Five thou initial bite, when things got tight another nip for five hundred more."

Kearny nodded. "What we need is somebody—Pete Gilmartin, maybe—who knows what she has on him. Whoever him is."

Heslip winked at Giselle. "Not Gilmartin. He's clean."

"You're sure?" Kearny demanded.

"Hell, Dan, the guy lives in a tract house. Two mortgages, first to the seller and second to Golden Gate Trust. One car—"

"No other real property?"

"Not in any Bay Area county. One car, he owes on it. Standard homeowner's and life insurance through one of the big Montgomery Street brokerage firms—Levinson Brothers in the Russ Building. Giselle ran a credit check on him. Paying on a color TV, washer-dryer. Good pay. Mastercharge with a $500 limit, owed $275 at the time checked. Wife, two kids, Little League . . ."

"Okay, I buy it," said Kearny, then made a liar of himself by asking, "Long-distance calls?"

"One a month to his folks back in Toledo. Two calls to an aunt in Cleveland—the wife's folks are local. I called the aunt myself—old-buddy-from-the-service routine. I could smell the apple pie."

"Why are you so thorough on Pete?" demanded Giselle.

"We need his help in getting a make on Nucci. How about some coffee, Giselle?"

They relaxed and chatted for ten minutes, then got back to it. Ballard ran through what he had already told Kearny about Padilla Trucking, and Kearny explained the significance of it and the fact that it smelled of Mafia. Then Ballard started on Nucci.

"Some of this I got; most of it Giselle got. He moved into the house on San Buenaventura in St. Francis Woods three years ago last month. But he doesn't own it."

Kearny sat up with a jerk. "Who the hell does?"

"An outfit calling itself Fraisa, Inc., are owner of record."

"Remember that name," said Giselle. "It's important."

"But Nucci pays the taxes," Ballard went on. "Purchase price was $175,000. First mortgage held by—"

"Golden Gate Trust?" asked Heslip.

"That's it," said Giselle. "I kept away from Golden Gate, Dan, so we don't know if the loan is legitimate—"

Kearny said, "It'll be legitimate. That isn't Nucci's division."

"We had a title company in South Lake Tahoe make a title search of the property in the Skyland development," said Ballard. "Fraisa, Inc., is also owner of record up there—little $65,000 'summer cottage.' They pay the taxes."

"I put that kid out of Truckee on it," Giselle put in, her clear blue eyes sparkling with excitement. "The place is used by a number of different groups, mainly businessmen with women the caretaker doubts are wives. Caretaker's year-round, retired Army, his wife does the cooking. They've got a detached bungalow."

"Is there a mortgage?" asked Kearny.

"Yeah," said Ballard. "Held by Padilla Trucking."

"Now we're getting someplace." Kearny went out to the postage-stamp kitchen for more coffee, came back making a face over it. "It's shaping up. Giselle, what have we got on Padilla Trucking?"

"You just *think* it's shaping up." She began consulting her typed notes. "California State Division of Corporations referred me to the

San Francisco Regional Office, which came up with the stockholders of record. Fraisa, Inc., and Marcello Supply Company of New York."

"Ring-around-the-rosy," muttered Kearny. "Of course, Marcello Supply will be the eastern money that funded the original deal."

"I wonder what they supply?" asked Ballard.

"Hoods out of New York," said Heslip.

"And the *officers* of Padilla?"

"The original board of directors was Frank Padilla, his wife Louisa, Nicolas DeSimone—the general manager of the trucking company—and . . . Jerry Garofolo."

The man who had hit Ed Dorsey. It reflected in all their faces. Kearny spoke first.

"DeSimone was probably the one who got away, then. And we can be pretty sure that they weren't moonlighting for anybody. It was organization business." He frowned, thinking deeply. "What's the stock split between Marcello Supply and Fraisa, Inc.?"

"Fifty-flve/forty-five."

"Who owns the Fraisa stock?" asked Heslip.

"Up until three years ago, Frank and Louisa Padilla. That's where the name comes from: F-r-a from Frank, i-s-a from Louisa."

"Three years," said Kearny quickly. "It was three years ago that Art Nucci—"

"Closed the deal on his house. Right. And on the same *day,* Art Nucci got ten percent of Fraisa's stock."

"Jackpot!" exclaimed Ballard.

"What we have to find out is what Nucci did to get it," said Kearny. "That's why we need Gilmartin's cooperation." He grinned. "Anyway, we have our connection. It's obvious that Frank Padilla is the one who ordered—"

"No," said Giselle. "N-o, no."

"What do you mean, no?"

"On the fifth of this month Frank Padilla's stock was transferred to a Mr. Philip Fazzino." She savored her moment of triumph. "Frank Padilla was killed in a car wreck on July twenty-second. Which was a week *before* Chandra got the five thousand dollars."

TEN

PETE GILMARTIN reached across the narrow table to take Giselle's hand. He conveyed it reverently to his lips. "I wish you'd told me we were coming to a Japanese restaurant," he murmured. "I've got a hole in my sock."

Giselle rescued her hand. "Nobody's liable to get down under the table and peek."

"Not under this table."

They were sitting in their stocking feet on the floor on opposite sides of the low hardwood rectangle, waiting for the Japanese waitress to arrive with the sukiyaki and sashimi.

Gilmartin looked regretfully into Giselle's very clear, very direct blue eyes. "I've never met a girl with so many *No trespassing* signs posted."

Giselle laughed with genuine amusement. It was a laugh to turn male heads. "The hell of it is, Pete, I like your wife and adore your kids. So there we are."

"You could at least *pretend* we've got an assignation in a plush upstairs room when our leisurely lunch is finished . . ."

"We might start to believe it," said Giselle lightly.

Gilmartin grinned his wide white grin. With his deep tan and greenish eyes, he looked like an adventurer rather than a banker. Before he could answer, the pixie-like waitress came in with a boardful of fresh vegetables for the *wok*. With proper ceremony, they ate, regretting the hot saké they'd decided to forgo in favor of headwork later that afternoon.

"Now," said Gilmartin firmly, when they'd reached the tea, "we shall get down to the *real* reason for this royal treatment. I know *you're* here because you're secretly, madly in love with me. But why is old hard-nose Kearny picking up the tab?"

"He wants you to abuse your position of trust at the bank to get into certain confidential financial records for us."

Gilmartin started to laugh heartily; stopped when Giselle did not join in; ended up just staring at her. He finally drew a deep breath and drummed the table with his fingertips.

"How many nontaxable dollars do I get for this little service?"

He tried to keep his voice light, but Giselle realized that Kearny had been right in detailing her to this task: it was just too subtle for him. It would have come out sounding like what Gilmartin was afraid it was.

"No money, Pete."

He relaxed in some fractional way. "Then it isn't just . . . business."

"The attack on Ed Dorsey was set up through somebody at your bank as an attempt on Dan."

Gilmartin drummed his fingertips again. "Wow!" he said softly at last. "Who at the bank?"

"We think Art Nucci."

"Who told me to get Dan up there at a certain time that evening. I see." He gave her a sudden wry smile. "Time to show the hole in my sock to the world."

When they were at the door, Gilmartin took the tall blonde's arm before she could slide open the flimsy bamboo-and-rice paper panel. "I report anything I find out to you?"

"Or to Dan."

She was almost as tall as he was; their faces were only inches apart. He leaned forward to brush her lips with his. "You make me feel like a little kid stealing a kiss in the coat-room, Giselle."

Walking down the stairs of the restaurant, Giselle caught herself hoping that he would report to Kearny, not her. Dammit, she *did* like Pete Gilmartin's wife and adore his kids, but she was beginning to find Pete himself an intensely exciting man.

*

Dan Kearny and Benny Nicoletti were eating bratwurst and kraut at the Rathskeller as Giselle and Gilmartin were leaving Nikko's nine blocks away.

Nicoletti cut the bloated sausage on his plate with the delicacy of a surgeon. Juice spurted out. "Remember I said Internal Affairs might be coming down on some of the boys doing little favors for people on the outside?"

Kearny nodded. It was their first reference to their last uncomfortable parting.

"They got a big Dutchman in Accident Division, inspector named Waterreus, under suspension. Accepting bribes from a couple of your competitors."

"Makes it easier for us." Kearny grinned.

Nicoletti changed the subject by pointing his fork at the detective. "I thought you didn't have no idea who might sic a couple of heavies on to one of your men."

"I don't. *You* mentioned Padilla Trucking . . . What was the disposition of the charge against Garofolo, anyway?"

Nicoletti drank dark beer, wiped away the foam mustache. "Arraigned last Friday. D.A. hit him with Assault with Intent to Commit Great Bodily Harm and bail was set at $35,000."

Kearny gave a silent whistle. "With no prior convictions? Pretty heavy."

"Not heavy enough. Old dude named Hawkley, counsel for Padilla Trucking, showed up with a tame bailbondsman who came up with it, cash money."

Kearny dipped a forkful of sauerkraut into the hot mustard on his plate. "Hawkley out of Concord, Walnut Creek, somewhere like that?"

"That's him. You know him?"

Kearny shook his head and lied. "Talked to him for five minutes once about a client of his we were looking for."

Wayne Hawkley, that tough old bird. Kearny had always thought there was something sour about his operation. In the past, nobody had been paying him to get curious about it. Now he was going to have to.

"You figure that Hawkley represents Padilla Trucking for more than just business problems?"

"Looks that way." Nicoletti belched with great gusto. "Why all this interest in Padilla Trucking?"

Kearny gestured almost angrily through the smoke of the cigarette he'd just lighted. "Aw, come on, Benny! One of my men gets flattened, you can bet your ass we're going to find out which way to be looking the next time. We nosed around a little, what we found pointed to Frank Padilla as one of the mob's local hotshots. Are we right?"

"Now how in hell would a hick cop know that, Dan?" He grinned, and went on in his high soft tenor, "*The* hotshot in Northern California, according to the state Organized Crime Squad."

"But he's dead. Went over Devil's Slide down on the coast in the fog a couple of months ago."

"Yeah. Last July. They fished the car out of the drink with him still in it. If you already knew he was dead, why was you asking—"

"I want to know who took his place."

"I'm s'posed to know?" Nicoletti looked at his watch. "Shit. I got a new partner, told him I'd meet him at your office fifteen minutes ago."

They stood up. Kearny scattered paper money on the table. "About this guy who took Padilla's place . . ."

Nicoletti sighed. "Second in command stepped up, according to rumor."

When he said nothing further, Kearny prodded, "He's got a name?"

"Fazzino, Phil Fazzino, they call him 'Flip'—behind his back."

Phil Fazzino. To whom Padilla's stock in Fraisa, Inc., had just been transferred. Fazzino. Was he the one Chandra was nipping?

"I'm glad none of these guys are Italian."

"Yeah," said Nicoletti placidly. "If they was, I might get an inferiority complex about my race."

"How did you make out with Pete?"

"What's that supposed to mean?"

Kearny observed the delicate flush mounting Giselle's cheeks. "Is he in or out?" he asked patiently.

"He'll do it for us."

"I'll bet he will," said Kearny.

"God*damn* you, Dan!" she burst out. Red now overlaid the usual cool ivory of her complexion.

Kearny's face became abruptly wooden. "Internal Affairs came down on Waterreus, hard," he said. "We backed off from him just in time."

The flush had begun fading from Giselle's features. Kearny was very busy lighting a cigarette. She reached across the desk to pluck one from the pack. Her mouth curved bitterly. "We wouldn't have to look very far for another cop to put on the payroll. That new partner of Benny's has his hand out." She tossed her heavy gleaming blond mane almost defiantly. She was a lovely woman. "I thought all these raises in cops' salaries were supposed to end all that."

"You make more, your standard of living goes up."

"Then you shouldn't be a cop."

"Besides, Benny probably put him up to it to see our reaction."

"Oh, wow!" Giselle, who seldom smoked, stubbed out a cigarette she'd just lighted. "What did you find out about Phil Fazzino?"

He'd learned a good deal. Fazzino was thirty-four, with a master's degree in business and an LL.B. from Harvard Law. Never practiced, had never been busted for anything, not even a traffic ticket, and of all things, was a chess player with a Master rating from FIDE. Whatever the hell FIDE was.

"He's had an office as a 'business consultant' down in the financial district for two years, was second-in-command in the organization when Padilla died. Benny says he's genuinely brilliant at business—which is why he's been able to move up so fast without ever having to get his hands dirty. What we need now is a connection between him and Chandra. We already have him connected to Nucci through joint stock ownership in Fraisa, Inc.—even though it's only by accident because Padilla died."

"Pete'll call me if he can find anything financial Nucci has done for either corporation." Giselle made herself meet Kearny's eyes casually as she said it. Damn him, what business of his was it if she enjoyed Pete's company? Nothing would come of it. She went on, "What do you want to do about Fazzino?"

"Put Larry on him. Loose tail."

"If he's jammed up on something else, will Bart—"

"Larry. I want him to get a good look at Fazzino cold, before he knows it's important." He shook out cigarettes for them both. Rapport was temporarily reestablished. "You know what bothers me, Giselle? With their manpower, they haven't put anybody on to *us*, you follow me? Makes our work easier, but I keep feeling it's important . . ."

Eleven

Pacific just beyond Steiner in Pacific Heights is a rich street. The only sounds to break the moneyed quiet are an occasional passing auto and the discreet mutter of a gardener's rake. City-planned but homeowner-financed trees shadow the street, lending the block an odd formality.

Larry Ballard was parked several doors down and across the street from 2416 when a child's delighted shriek jerked his head up. He looked quickly around, momentarily disoriented. A boy just past the toddler stage was running by the Plymouth's misted side window on stubby legs, pursued by a laughing miniskirted nurse who swept him up in her arms. In bending, the girl gave Ballard a long tempting moment of buttocks through nearly transparent pantyhose. He watched with carnal lust.

Jesus, he thought, shaking the last of the cobwebs out of his head, if Dan had come along and found him half asleep . . .

But five hours here, nobody in or out of the house. He leaned forward to peer at it again through the moisture-beaded windshield. It was deceptively large, set back from the street behind head-high, impeccably trimmed hedges. A black filigree iron gate was set in the side of the hedge toward the driveway.

Ballard leaned forward, his muscular body tense. A gray Jaguar sedan, long and sleek and shiny despite the failing light and the mist, was turning in. California plates 626 ZFF. A blonde behind the wheel who probably was young and pretty, but he couldn't be sure.

With sudden decision Ballard got out to stroll down his side of the street until he could see past the hedge on the near side of the driveway. The garage door, twenty feet wide and inset under a first-floor wing of the house, was just going up. The Jag went through, the door started down. Two minutes later lights went on in the house.

Ballard was back in his car and the streetlights were burning when a second car turned in at 2416. It stopped in the driveway with enough of the rear end sticking out from behind the hedge for him to see 843 MCW. A new Ford Gran Torino.

The driver came around the back of the car to go up the walk toward the arched portico over the front entryway. The front door was decorated with a massive brass knocker, but he used a key.

He moved like a cat. Ballard couldn't see his suit under the genuine Burberry trenchcoat he wore, but was sure it would be magnificent. No wonder that sly bastard Kearny had specified him to pull surveillance at this address! He'd seen the man before, and Kearny had suspected it. At South Park, getting out of a red Caddy convertible.

"His name is Phil Fazzino," said Giselle, "and he holds the pink on the Gran Torino." She was drinking Scotch, which she didn't really like, because Pete Gilmartin had ordered it for her. "But the Jaguar—"

"Allow me to astound you." Gilmartin spoke with something of a flourish. "The gray Jaguar sedan, California 626 ZFF, is registered to none other than Mr. Arthur Nucci, vice-president of . . ."

"Golden Gate Trust, through which it is financed," finished Giselle. "So I'm not astounded after all."

Reddish light from the fireplace danced on her face, blushing warm tones into her skin. She knew she was talking too much, like a girl on her first date, but she couldn't help it. Huge, beautifully ornate chandeliers sparkled above them.

Shirley, the lovely cocktail waitress who was also one of the owners of Rocca's, stopped at their table. "Another round, kids?"

"Of course," said Gilmartin. "Then we'll want dinner—"

"No, Pete, we . . ."

But Shirley had departed, tipping Giselle an approving wink behind Pete's back. She and Giselle were old friends, Rocca's had seemed ideal for keeping it a business rather than personal rendezvous. It wasn't working out that way.

"Pete, I didn't mean for dinner! I just thought . . ."

"I've got *much* too much to tell you over a couple of drinks." Gilmartin flashed his engaging grin, and said in a serious voice, "Some of it's even about Art Nucci."

"Pete, please . . ."

Kearny glanced at Giselle's face as Gilmartin talked. She was watching the banker avidly. You could always tell, Kearny thought, even without the fact that she hadn't been home to change clothes since yesterday. Not just by the face and the eyes. Somehow the body itself had a softer, rounder, almost fuller look.

He shut it off. Gilmartin, explaining the photocopied records he had spread out on Kearny's desk, was giving them a lot of answers.

"The first loan to Padilla Trucking was approved by Nucci for Golden Gate Trust three years ago September. For $28,000. Seven months later there was a second loan for $27,000."

"Also to the corporation?" asked Kearny.

"That's right." Gilmartin's lean face was enthusiastic as he paced the narrow space between the desk and the partially opened glass door. "But between that second loan to the corporation and Padilla's death last August, there were four *more* loans, totaling $50,000. These were personal loans to Frank Padilla, secured with Fraisa stock."

"All together, $105,000 in three years," mused Kearny. He turned to Giselle. "Do we have any indication of what the assets of Padilla Trucking and Fraisa, Inc., really are?"

Giselle was leafing through her file. "I don't think . . ."

The sliding door opened further. Larry Ballard stuck his head in. "Dan! That chick is . . ."

Kearny was on his feet, cutting in smoothly, "Larry, good timing. We were just wondering what sort of plant Padilla Trucking has."

"Uh . . . It's a hell of a big yard, Dan. Jammed with equipment, but how much of that they own and how much—"

"Yeah." Kearny turned to Gilmartin. "Golden Gate call in those loans when Padilla died? The personal ones, backed with Fraisa stock?"

Gilmartin shook his head. "That's the first thing a financial institution *always* does when a debtor dies, Dan, but Golden Gate merely renegotiated them with a man named Phil Fazzino. On . . . let's see . . ." He looked up from the photocopies on the desk. "On the fifth of this month."

Kearny nodded. He said nothing of the fact that this was the same day that the dead Padilla's stock had been transferred to Fazzino. Instead he pumped Gilmartin's hand warmly, up and down. "You don't know how happy we are, Pete, to have you on our team."

"I'll be in touch through Giselle," said Gilmartin with his widest grin, wide enough to give the remark a veiled double meaning. He turned to the slender blonde. "Walk me out to my car, kid."

Ballard stared broodingly after them, then turned back to Kearny with a slight shrug, as if rejecting not particularly welcome thoughts. "The blonde's name is Wendy Austin."

"That was fast work."

"I got lucky. At ten this morning I tailed her to a boutique in that big new office building on Union Street out in Cow Hollow. The one with the underground parking. Wendy's Funky Threads, far-out men's and women's clothes at out-of-sight prices. I snooped through the display windows, saw her ordering around the salesgirl, so after I'd tailed her to a beauty shop I called the boutique and asked for Wendy Fazzino."

"You mean she's his *wife?*" demanded Kearny, surprised.

"No. The chick at the boutique said I must want Wendy *Austin*."

"Good work. I'll see if Benny Nicoletti can find a pedigree on her."

When Ballard was gone, Kearny rang Giselle's station in the clerical offices overhead. He told her he was leaving early, had something to check in the East Bay, and told her what to pass on to Nicoletti. He hesitated, then plunged into the part he had to say but didn't want to. "Ah . . . Giselle, I don't want Pete Gilmartin to have access to anything DKA is doing on the Chandra case."

Immediate anger hardened her voice. "What's that supposed to mean, Dan?"

"What I said. I don't give a damn what you do on your own time, but Larry and Bart are damned vulnerable in the field right now. I trust Pete's discretion, but I want to be *sure.* You got that?"

"Goddammit, Dan, do you think I'd—"

"You *got that?*"

There was a long pause. Tears glinted in her voice when she finally answered, "I've got it."

He slammed down the phone and stood beside the desk, breathing deeply, as if he had been running. Finally he uttered a short, ugly blasphemy and went around the desk toward the door. Women and their goddam emotions.

TWELVE

WAYNE E. HAWKERY'S law offices were in Concord, an East Bay community some twenty miles east of Oakland. A quiet side street in a quiet town, drowsy in the late-fall heat; a town caught unprepared for the scores of miles of subdivisions which had sprung up around it since World War II.

Kearny parked across from the one-story cinder-block building, then sat in the wagon for a few moments, staring at the red-brick façade and the plate-glass windows reflecting afternoon sunlight. Six months ago he'd wanted only an address from Hawkley. Now he wanted much more—and was going to have a tough time getting it.

"Good afternoon, Mr. Kearny." The lean dark intense secretary wore rimless glasses and still had good legs and still showed a lot of them.

"You're very good, Maddy," he said.

A smile curved the girl's thin lips without touching the eyes behind the bland glasses. "You're very good yourself, Mr. Kearny, remembering a lowly secretary's name. But it's *Ms. Hawkley* except to friends."

"Is the old gentleman available?"

He watched her slender back disappear down the passageway to her grandfather's private office. He wished that he had her backstopping Giselle. Giselle. Dammit, if only he'd mentioned Gilmartin's steady stream of shack-ups to her sometime, just in passing. A hell of a good banker, Gilmartin, pragmatic and very bright. But a sexual son of a bitch despite his wife and two sons.

Or perhaps because of them?

Anyway, Giselle would rip her guts out thinking she had led him astray from home and family. She just wasn't the kind for casual flops in the pad with a married man.

"Right this way, please, Mr. Kearny."

Old Wayne Hawkley still smoked long expensive cigars and still drank the best bourbon there was. He was just bringing the bottle and two shot glasses from the drawer of the old-fashioned roll-top desk when Kearny was ushered in.

He stuck his cigar in his mouth to free a hand for Kearny's, took it out again to say, "That'll be all, Maddy."

Clear blue eyes that were at least a generation younger than the lean brown face regarded Kearny sardonically through old-fashioned spectacles. The thin lips quirked. "I was wondering when you'd honor us with a visit."

"That so?" Kearny sat down, thinking that he'd have to chew out Heslip and Ballard for missing the tags Hawkley had put on them.

"Once I appeared to represent Mr. Garofolo, I figgered it was just a matter of time."

So. No tags, just foresight. Kearny knew that under the sparse shoe-polish-black hair a computer brain to challenge his own was flashing away. He drank, Hawkley poured. Wild Turkey died an easy death.

The lawyer said mildly, "I *am* on retainer to Garofolo's employer, you know. It's only natural, when he's in trouble . . ."

Kearny got out his filtered Camels. The Surgeon General had finally scared him that much. Time went by. They sipped and smoked.

Hawkley finally sighed. "I take it you've discovered my client's youthful indiscretions."

Kearny set down his empty shot glass. "He's an enforcer," he said. On the wall behind the roll-top desk was Hawkley's framed certificate announcing that he had been admitted to the California State Bar in 1927. "So I thought I'd drop around, find out if I should send my family out of town."

Hawkley made an abrupt, almost alarmed gesture with one big, gnarled hand. "Now dammit, Mr. Kearny, ain't no need to take that tone. You know very well that your Mr. Dorsey was mistaken for—"

"For me?"

Hawkley stared at him almost blankly for several seconds. The "ain't" was artful, Kearny knew, something developed originally for the juries which had become habitual. Old-fashioned watch chain across the lean belly, carefully calculated folksiness, the slips in grammar—all programmed for jury-appeal.

"I declare," said Hawkley at last. He leaned back to laugh in genuine delight. It was not an old man's laugh, though he had to carry at least as many decades as the century. "May I be frank, Mr. Kearny?"

"That's why I'm here."

"Well, between you and me, Jerry Garofolo sometimes does favors for a friend who has a modest financial undertaking—"

"Jesus!" burst in Kearny. "Being frank? He's an enforcer for a shylocker—six bucks a week for every five, with lots of sweet loans to push the vigorish up."

"I prefer financial undertaking," said Hawkley dryly. "In any event, Mr. Garofolo and his associate not only had the wrong man—Mr. Dorsey *did* bear a superficial resemblance to the . . . um . . . delinquent debtor—but they used much more force than the occasion required . . ."

Which bothered Kearny. The old bastard sounded as if he was telling the truth when he said that Ed Dorsey was hit by accident, pure and simple, by a couple of the syndicate's loan-shark enforcers. It explained why nobody from the Mafia was taking any interest in Kearny's field men. But it didn't explain what Chandra had on the syndicate worth five thousand bucks. It didn't explain the threatening phone call. It didn't explain Fazzino's paying off Chandra personally. Hawkley could be lying of course, but . . .

A possible way to find out. "I'd be interested in knowing whether Garofolo's going to show up for his trial."

"Jump bail?" Hawkley looked shocked, much too shocked to actually be shocked. "Padilla Trucking has put up a $35,000 cash bond to ensure—"

"Is he?"

Hawkley drew a deep breath. "He . . . um . . . accepted an assignment overseas on the day of his release on bail."

So the syndicate would eat the thirty-five thou. Which meant he *had* been on mob business, which, goddammit, just didn't make sense. Yet.

"You've eased my mind a good deal," he said to Hawkley untruthfully.

The range of hills between Oakland and Contra Costa County meant that neither San Francisco nor Oakland Control could reach the small radio unit in Kearny's car. He reached home in Lafayette fifteen minutes after leaving Hawkley's office, and went straight through to the bedroom. In the closet was a big radio sender/receiver with a range almost equal to that of KDM 366 Control in San Francisco. He called Giselle.

"Any word from our contact downtown, over?"

"Negative, SF-1."

"Have him call me here if he has anything."

Kearny changed into old clothes to go out and mow the lawn. He wondered unhappily whether he might have to yank Giselle off the case entirely. Intensely loyal people, once deflected from the person or organization which had their loyalty . . .

And what was more calculated to confuse a girl of relatively little sexual experience than an intense love affair with a lot of nice gooey guilt mixed up in it?

He went up the hall past the empty kids' rooms and through the big kitchen, remembering that brooding look Ballard had sent after Giselle and Gilmartin. There was a nonphysical intimacy between Ballard and Giselle which might be useful . . .

The phone rang. He answered it on the first ring; Jeanie had planned to take the kids down to get decorations for the Hallowe'en party on the way home from school and wasn't home yet.

"Dan? I didn't find nothing on that little Austin girl for you here," came Benny Nicoletti's soft, almost apologetic voice.

"That tells us something in itself, Benny."

"But I did get sort of a line on her. Just for the hell of it, I took a look through the Juvenile Court Index—those records are sealed, the Index just tells you *who's* been sealed, you understand? There ain't no way to get into the file itself without a court order; but I gotta contact or two in the juvie probation setup. One of 'em *thinks* he remembers it was something to do with skin-flicks. Thinks she was maybe seventeen at the time, the filmmaker got busted for Contributing under W and I six hundred."

W&I 600: a statute of the Welfare and Institutions Code.

"Dependent Children, Benny?"

"That's it. He can't remember what happened to the girl, probably probation under control of the parents or something. Maybe three, four years ago. Like I said, otherwise she's clean."

Kearny stood in abstraction after thanking him and hanging up. Benny was being damned accommodating all of a sudden, bending rules he'd usually only bend in the interest of what the SFPD saw as justice.

Time to quit using him as a bird dog. What the hell was the name of that friend of Bart's who . . . Yeah, Bob McDade, that was it. Get Bart to ask him if he'd ever heard of Wendy Austin. They had to establish the connection between Fazzino and Chandra; it *could* be through the girl. McDade, who was into that whole porn-movie scene, might know something about her.

THIRTEEN

WENDY AUSTIN was an incredibly beautiful girl. Her blue eyes looked up into those of the black man standing beside the bed; her full lips, bright and gleaming, were parted in anticipation and her tongue came out over her small white even teeth. Her blond hair made a glistening halo on the pillow.

Then his naked black body covered hers; her arms tightened about his shoulders as her full breasts cushioned under his weight. Her beautifully sculpted legs accepted him.

Wendy Austin began to talk. A stream of almost clinically scatalogical terms spewed from her, dainty at first, then becoming coarser as she urged him on to greater effort and sweat darkened the sheet beneath her. Finally her fingernails began raking thin bloody gashes down his back.

"She was seventeen then," said Bob McDade.

The moving Technicolor images on the beaded screen faded as the room lights came up. Bart Heslip was sweating. He went to the heavily screened window of the projection booth to look down through dirt-crusted glass at Sixth Street. A white drunk was standing on the sidewalk below, head back, drinking muscatel. It was three in the afternoon.

"Baby, ain't she something?" persisted McDade to his back.

McDade was a big black man, coal-black, with a fuzzy Afro and wearing the extreme in hip clothes. A knife scar ran down across his throat beneath his shirt collar. He was still alive because years ago

Heslip had kept a thumb pressed on the artery during a wild-ass ride to the hospital.

"We made four of those with her, three, three and a half years ago. Each time she took us all on afterwards—me, the cameraman, the sound man—"

"What'd you pay her?"

"Same as everybody—twenty-five a picture. Wanta see the rest of 'em?"

"I couldn't take it," said Heslip truthfully, feeling a faint revulsion.

Bob McDade had come out of the government housing projects at Hunter's Point, same as Heslip, had started out making quickie pornos in pads rented from landlords who knew the tenant would be at work for the afternoon. Now he owned two skin-flick houses, a grocery/liquor store three doors away, a men's clothing store, a $60,000 house over in Richmond and an expensive Danish wife to whom he was unfaithful with every girl appearing in one of his films.

"You still showing these?" asked Heslip.

McDade's face closed up like a fist. "Don't jive me, man. You ain't that goddam dumb."

"Maybe not." Heslip started for the door, then turned to point at the film. "But you are."

"Sheeit, baby, private stock, purely—for my own solitary sorrowful gazin' an' rememberin'."

"Know where I can find her now? It's important."

McDade said thoughtfully, "No idea, man. I remember she was takin' voice and elocution and dancing lessons . . . Hell, I remember her wanting us to do one with her as Marilyn Monroe, she had that voice down perfect, and . . ."

"Thanks a lot, baby," snapped Heslip.

"Man, I *told* you I dunno! Maybe, you really need to find her, you got to *act,* or somebody . . ."

"Don't jive *me,* man," said Heslip softly. "Maybe Flippo would like to see this print."

Pure terror spasmed McDade's face. He came quickly to the door and grabbed Heslip's arm. "You ain't seen this, man! Promise me! He know I still got these, it be my black ass, surely."

Heslip went away without promising. McDade owed him, then came around with that I-dunno shit. Let him sweat it for a day or two.

Giselle leaned back in her chair and blew smoke out through her nostrils. She had smoked more in the past few days than in the whole month. It was that damn Kearny and his ability to reach into her mind and grab out what she was thinking. What made it worse, *she* didn't know what she was thinking; everything was a whirl and a muddle. She hated it, yet could hardly wait for the workday to end so she could get to Rocca's to meet Peter. And then . . .

Other, more intimate images of the inevitable end of the evening flooded over her, making her body feel heated with anticipation.

How in hell had it happened to her? So suddenly, so completely? Pete's lovely wife, and the two boys, seven and nine years old—three months ago she'd spent half the company picnic walking those kids around the Lafayette Reservoir. If there were someone she could *talk* to . . .

Larry? She would completely panic trying to tell him about it. Bart? O'B? Nobody. No . . .

Kearny came in with his empty coffee cup dangling from a finger.

"Mr. Gilmartin phoned," Giselle said formally as the telltale flush mounted her cheeks. "He's giving us a re-open on Chandra."

"The hell! You *sure?*" Kearny seemed thunderstruck.

"With a *Hold* until a week from Wednesday. He's going to send out Final Notice on Friday if she doesn't pick up the delinquent payment this week."

"Dammit, Giselle, it just don't reach." Kearny was pacing. "If you see Pete tonight, ask him if this is his idea or Nucci's."

"He already told me. Nucci's."

"Did Bart find out if Fazzino had ever seen those films of his girl friend?"

"He asked McDade that." Giselle suddenly found herself giggling. "He said McDade turned white."

Just then Heslip's voice came over the radio: "SF-3 calling KDM 366."

"This is KDM 366. Go ahead."

"Subject appears headed toward vicinity Grant and Greenwich."

"10-4. Stand by." She released the *Transmit* button. "He's tailing Wendy Austin, and she—"

"I heard." Kearny's voice betrayed no excitement, but the gray eyes were alive with it. "There's our link, Giselle. Wendy Austin. How long does somebody work out at a dance studio like that?"

"A serious student, about two hours."

"Okay. Tell him that if she—"

Heslip's voice broke in again. "Subject just parked on Lombard Street by Julius Alley. That's a confirm on the destination."

Kearny had been quietly smoking behind the wheel of the station wagon for twenty minutes when the beautifully shaped blonde unlocked the Jaguar. She was wearing only a black leotard and black tights under her open coat, giving him a glimpse of her remarkable body as she got into the low-slung sports car. She had her street clothes over her arm. No showers in that place?

As Kearny trudged up narrow Grant Avenue, Heslip's Plymouth passed him going down. Neither man gave a flicker of recognition. Far below, the lights of the piers jutting out from the Embarcadero had been blotted out by a fog bank that had the horns crying out in the bay.

Lights inside Chandra's studio made the uneven brush strokes stand out on the glass of door and window. He went in. Light classical music came from a cheap portable record player set on a straight-back chair in one corner. Chandra was nowhere around.

"I'd like to talk with someone about lessons for my daughter," he told a limber serious-faced girl who was standing with her head down, panting.

"That'd be . . . Chandra, but I guess . . . she bugged out . . ." She caught her breath. "Sometimes she splits for half an hour or so . . ."

But just then Chandra emerged from a curtained doorway in the plasterboard partition which stretched across the back of the studio. The curtain was a faded green. Chandra herself was a small broad figure in black leotard and tights. She had the legs and hips of a dock worker, oddly combined with a fluid grace so ingrained as to be unconscious.

"Support, Norman!" she cried. A man and woman had just flitted by in tandem, the woman wearing a long split skirt over her leotards and tights. The man had better legs. Chandra cried after them, "You're not giving her enough support for her pirouette, Norman!"

"The unmannerly bastard," said Kearny. "I waited until Wendy left before I came in."

"Oh!" She had whirled to stare up at him from vividly faded blue eyes. "You startled me!" Then her gravelly voice belatedly added, "Wendy who?"

"Fazzino's girl friend. Anywhere we can talk? Your car's going to be assigned to us again in ten days."

Her face momentarily sagged. "But I just . . ." Then she caught herself. "I'll . . . take care of it by then."

"Don't do it, Chandra. Give it up."

She realized she wasn't going to get rid of him, so she heaved a long-suffering sigh. "The dressing room, then."

They crossed to the partition. The studio was shabby, dingy, the floor unswept.

"They come to dance, not make beds of roses and a thousand fragrant posies," she said defensively to his unspoken distaste. Then she shot an almost coquettish look at him, as if assessing his reaction to her quote.

He gave a heavy, sardonic chuckle. "Don't try to con me, lady. Hell's Kitchen—remember? I don't give a damn about fragrant posies, but does it have to smell like a hamper full of old jockstraps?"

"People sweat and sweat gets stale. At least I scrub the shower stall down with Lysol twice a week—that's more than most of 'em do." She stopped so abruptly at the curtain that Kearny bumped into her. She yelled, "Watch your turnout! Your *turn*-ou . . . that's better."

A slight flat-chested girl holding one of the bars along the wall with one hand, while doing what looked to Kearny like deep knee bends, changed the position of her feet. Chandra nodded approvingly.

The cubicle was empty. Bare hooks were screwed into the walls at about chin-height over the single long gray wooden bench. The back partition ended short of the left wall, so it was possible to walk around the end of it.

Chandra faced Kearny defiantly. "I have no intention of giving up my car," she said.

He sat down on the bench. Even sitting, he didn't have to look up at her very much. "What do you have on them and how did you get it?"

"I don't know what you're talking about."

"Cut it out, Chandra," he said in a pained voice. "It has to be heavy for a five-thou first bite. You got panicky when the bank said they were assigning the car to a repo agency, and hit Fazzino for another five hundred. Now you're thinking of trying it again. Don't."

Anger, fear, curiosity—all were fighting in her lined face. He realized that she was a little girl trapped in an aging body. He wanted to take her by the shoulders and shake her.

"This isn't a game, Chandra!" he snapped. "One man's already in the hospital, and—"

A lean muscular girl with unexpectedly large and slightly sagging breasts came from behind the rear partition, her head buried in a fuzzy towel. Water beaded her totally nude body. Her face emerged as she lowered her arms, and she saw them for the first time. She had beautiful copper-colored hair. "Sorry," she said vaguely.

She reached for underclothes, making no attempt to cover her well-shaped dancer's body in the meantime. The muscles of her belly and thighs had good separation.

"About half the kids wait to shower when they get home," said Chandra as if in explanation of the redhead.

Like Wendy Austin, thought Kearny. He stood in the doorway, looking stolidly out at the dance floor. For himself, not for the redhead. To her, a stray man in the dressing room was just another set of clothes like those hanging on the hooks. He counted a dozen dancers and four or five people in street clothes waiting for them to finish.

"Who's in the hospital?" Chandra demanded when the red-haired girl, now dressed and wearing an old raincoat, had departed.

Kearny told her: who, and how, and—as far as DKA was concerned—why. When he had finished he stood in front of her, legs set, hands thrust deep into his topcoat pockets.

"Don't try pushing them again, Chandra. You know damned well they're the sort that pushes back. Just give up the car and—"

"I won't!" she exclaimed. In a quieter voice, she went on, "It's beautiful, the most beautiful thing I've ever . . . Why, to me, that car is . . ."

"Is it worth dying for?" he asked softly.

FOURTEEN

THAT WAS Thursday night. On the following Wednesday, Fazzino stuck his head through the open doorway. A table had been shoved up against it to serve as a reception desk.

"Philip Fazzino to see Daniel Kearny," he called over to Giselle.

"Mr. Kearny asked that you go right down to his private office."

"Clairvoyance?" Harvard Law still slightly broadened the vowels in his well-modulated voice. Then his eyes touched the big radio and he nodded. "Of course. Radio-controlled units."

"If you'd go back down the stairs, sir, and into the garage, you'll find Mr. Kearny's office at the very back."

Fazzino, as Larry had said, was indeed handsome in an almost sculpted way. His softly waved hair just touched the tops of his ears and the back of his collar. Only his dark eyes were jarring: pellets of lead, with absolutely no depths. He smiled at her winningly. "I understand this place used to be a whorehouse."

"That's right." Giselle made her voice saccharine.

He kept those flat eyes fixed on her face. "Why don't you drop your panties, slut, so I can see what you're selling?"

Giselle laughed aloud. She clapped her hands in delight. "Why, that's *perfect,* Mr. Fazzino! George Raft? Ah . . . no, no, I have it. Jimmy Cagney! Ah . . . no! Mickey Rooney doing Andy Hardy!"

Fazzino's face turned to stone. He walked rapidly back down the hall toward the head of the stairs. Giselle started trembling. Her face was burning. For the first time she realized the sort of control field men had to have when they were being baited.

"He's on his way," she choked into the intercom.

"Have Bart come in too, Giselle."

Fazzino ignored Kearny's outstretched hand. He looked around and sat down, totally at his ease.

"So the big private eye spends his time hiding in the basement."

"Did you wish to hire the services of our firm, Mr. Fazzino?"

Fazzino leaned forward slightly. "I want you off my back."

"Subject to state and federal statutes, anyone can investigate anyone he wishes, Mr. Fazzino. Ah! Mr. Heslip! Come in, I want you to meet—"

Fazzino cast a contemptuously casual look over his shoulder. "I don't like niggers," he said coldly. "Give him a plate of ribs and get him out of here."

Kearny drew in a sharp breath; he'd seen Bart bust heads for much less. But Heslip was lounged against the aluminum doorframe, his hands in his pockets and his eyes rolled up toward the ceiling.

"Yassuh, boss," he said vaguely to the acoustical tiles. "Go see me some mo' dem' mo'on pichurs. Seen one yist'day, li'l ol' gal name of Wendy Austin was ballin' dis hyar big black stud, an' dat stud . . ."

With a strangled exclamation, Fazzino was on his feet, his eyes scummy with rage. "Where did you see that film?" he snarled.

Heslip continued to stare vacantly at the ceiling. Fazzino growled and lunged forward, hands outstretched to seize the front of his shirt. With incredible speed, Heslip skipped back from his grasp.

Then Heslip's right hand came out of his pocket. His forefinger, slowly becoming rigid as the arm straightened, pointed at Fazzino's stomach. In some odd way it was as menacing as an open switchblade. The tip of the finger began making a tight circle. "Open, honky," he said softly. "You mess wid me, man, dat's all-l-l gonna be *open* in dere." Then his mouth suddenly gaped idiotically. "Ah saw dat mo'on pichur, Ah mos' surely *did.* Dey was showin' it down at de Vice Squad. Dey call it a *trainin'* fillum on how to rec'nize hookers."

Fazzino looked from one to the other, as if memorizing their faces. There was cold fury in his eyes. "You're dead," he said. "You're both dead."

He went by Heslip and was gone, not without a certain restrained elegance. It was tough to *not* be elegant in a suit like that.

"Keep on him," snapped Kearny. Then, as Heslip started out, he added, "Don't follow him up any dead-end alleys, Bart."

Heslip's black face broke into a grin. "Yassuh, boss."

Kearny leaned back in his creaky swivel chair, his cigarette drifting smoke toward the ceiling. "What did you think, Giselle?" he asked the empty room.

Her voice—with laughter in it—came through the open intercom. "I don't think he knew what hit him, Dan."

"Yeah," rumbled Kearny. "Blew his cool, acted like a punk, uttered stupid threats . . . Only it just don't fit with what we've heard about this cat, you follow me?"

"Well . . . yes, but ... I think Bart got to him, and . . ."

"Dammit, Giselle." He tapped a clenched fist on his desk. "I've just got a feeling something's going to happen that we won't like . . ."

But for five days nothing happened. Not until Monday.

Well, actually, quite a bit happened over that weekend, but most of it was sexual and none of it had to do with Flip Fazzino.

Pete Gilmartin, on Friday, told his wife there was a bankers' convention in L.A. and then asked Giselle to go down to Carmel with him for the weekend. He told her he loved her and wanted to marry her as soon as he could figure out how to tell his wife—who, as Giselle knew, was depressed and talking suicide. Giselle, who *hadn't* known, cried and felt guilty and said she loved him too. And went to Carmel.

On Saturday night Ballard was very close to making Maria Navarro when one of Maria's daughters came out of the bedroom crying for a drink of water. Then *Maria* burst out crying. God frowned, she said, because what they had almost done was a sin without marriage. And her with two goddam kids. Ballard drove home vowing never to go out with a Catholic again.

Heslip sneaked over to see Corinne on Sunday morning despite Kearny's prohibitions, after making damn sure somebody *didn't* have a tag on him. Corinne wormed out of him, in ways not approved by

Women's Lib, what was really going on. First she was scared, then she was mad, so it took until almost midnight to make up. They kept making up repeatedly for the rest of the night, so Heslip went into work on Monday morning completely shot.

Also on Sunday, in the afternoon, Bob McDade wrapped up the third porno quickie he'd made with a rather razzle-dazzle brunette, then when he got home, discovered he had caught a dose of clap from that same leading lady at the *first* film session. Since it had taken seven days to become manifest, he had already passed it on to his blond Danish wife. Who, since she knew *she* hadn't been messing around, threw him out.

Dan Kearny finished mowing the lawn.

Fazzino's usual route to his financial district office was to pop down to Broadway, go through the tunnel to Columbus, hang a right to Montgomery and park in his rented stall. So Heslip was just sort of loafing along behind, thinking yeah, *man,* that Corinne Jones could sure make a little black detective feller hate to get up and go to work in the morning, when . . .

What the hell?

Fazzino had gone right by his building and across torn-up Market Street, had taken a right off New Montgomery—proving he wasn't headed for the freeway.

"Subject vehicle outbound on Mission, over," Heslip told the newly installed radio. He was driving a repo with Minnesota plates which DKA had decided to pick up as a company car.

Kearny himself answered—probably up there getting a cup of that bug juice he called coffee. "Think he made the tail, SF-3?"

"Negative. I'm in that Olds with foreign plates we just put the radio into, 366. And I picked him up at Franklin and Broadway instead of his house."

"Do you want another unit to front-tail, over?"

"Negative, 366. I . . . Subject slowing at green zone in front of Main Post Office, he's going to . . . No. Subject turning into Seventh Street . . ."

Which was one-way inbound to Market. Fazzino dawdled along in the left lane in front of the Greyhound terminal, with his emergency blinker on to indicate a double-park. Heslip, half a block behind, was craning out of his window in front of an old pensioners' hotel as if waiting for someone, in case Fazzino was using his rear-view mirror.

That's when Fazzino goosed it.

Heslip realized just too late that he had actually been timing the lights on Market so he could cross on the yellow. He did.

Heslip had to sit through the red.

"SF-3 to KDM 366 Control. Subject doused the tail. Repeat, subject doused tail."

Which told Kearny that the tail had been spotted and deliberately lost. His reaction was much stronger than Heslip had expected. "Go directly to Chandra's residence, SF-3. Confirm that she is there and stick with her. I don't care if you have to ride around in that Cadillac with her, *don't let anything happen to her.*"

Heslip crossed Market, goosed the Olds up Leavenworth, grimly cursing himself for being suckered by Fazzino. *Especially* by Fazzino. If Kearny was so worried, maybe they ought to call in the cops . . .

Yeah. And tell them what?

The radio cleared its throat. "KDM 366 to SF-6. What is your 10-20? SF-6, what is your 10-20, over?"

Ballard's voice came back almost immediately. "Going down the hill on Steiner, just turning east into Union Street. Subject appears en route to Funky Threads, over."

Heslip looked automatically at his watch. Eight-forty in the morning? Wendy Austin had never gotten to that shop before ten o'clock since they had started tailing her. What the hell went on?

"Maintain surveillance, SF-6," said Kearny's voice. "Overt, if necessary not to lose subject."

"10-4," said Ballard. Who would have heard Heslip and Control talking, of course, and so would already know that DKA was out of contact with Flip Fazzino.

They were well and truly into it now, Heslip thought.

FIFTEEN

AFTER SPOTTING the big red Caddy street-parked on Child, a little half-block alley above Grant, Heslip left his car and trotted up the slanting concrete walk between nearly waist-high foliage. He didn't stop at Chandra's front door, however, but continued on down the side of the house to check out the yard. It was choked with a wild profusion of shrubbery and old bushy gnarled miniature trees a dozen feet high which kept out the morning sunlight. The whole yard was enclosed by a solid wooden fence the same height as the trees.

No door cut in it. Which meant she came out by the front steps or not at all. Good. Made his job easier.

She opened the door to his knocking. "Yes?"

"Just checking." He left, feeling her puzzled eyes on his back.

And until dawn the next day, that was that. She left the house only twice, once to go down the hill to the Napoli Market, the other to trudge up the hill to her studio. On neither foray did she seem to be looking for or to notice Heslip across the street in his car.

In which he spent a miserable night.

Giselle spent the night in ecstasy with Petie, result of his call to inform DKA that final notice had gone out to Chandra the previous Friday morning. He instructed DKA to pick up the Caddy on Wednesday unless he told them different, and instructed Giselle to meet him at Rocca's after work. If the car *was* repo'ed, the account would be declared in jeopardy and final payoff demanded. Giselle already knew what would happen if she met him after work.

Larry Ballard's night, also in his car, equaled Bart's for misery. Only it was spent 335 miles south, in Santa Barbara.

Leaving the underground garage of the building her boutique was in at 2:00 P.M., Wendy Austin had turned right instead of left, and had just kept going. Ballard had unclipped his mike.

"Subject taking Turk Street on-ramp to Skyway."

Giselle's voice came back loud and clear from the office just a block away. "Don't lose her, Hotshot."

"This is SF-6, not SF-3."

Which ought to make Bart's day, he grinned to himself.

The Jag went south toward San Jose, not east toward the Bay Bridge. When they had passed the Cow Palace cutoff, Ballard radioed he was leaving the city. This time Kearny was on the radio.

"She trying to run away from you, SF-6?"

"Holding a steady sixty-eight, over."

"Report by phone if she takes you out of radio range."

She took him out of radio range. The Bayshore Freeway runs down the west side of the Bay, through the connected string of peninsula towns which expanding population has congealed into one long narrow strip of urban sprawl, and she ran right through all of it. Passing the giant gray hangars of Moffett Field, Ballard radioed DKA his last report with a wing of Navy jets screaming by overhead and his voice transmission breaking up.

Eight miles south of San Jose they lost the freeway where town after dusty valley town dropped speeds to forty-five, thirty-five, twenty-five. School zone, fifteen miles an hour. Coyote. Madrone. Morgan Hill—with stoplights, yet.

Finally Gilroy, with the westering sun glinting off hot chrome. Ballard closed up to three blocks, in case she tried to slip into California 152 where it trudged up through Pacheco Pass to Interstate 5.

She stayed on 101. Open highway again, with twilight making things glimmer. South of the Watsonville cutoff he had to switch on his lights. She held a steady sixty-eight, sixty-nine, a good smart driver—CHP would give you seventy before they ticketed you.

Meanwhile, Ballard had started to get worried. Those Jags had big tanks, she might just run him down to *Empty* and lose him without even knowing it. But at the Airport Road turnoff a few miles south of Salinas, she flicked on her turn signal. Whew. Salinas was the last large town until San Luis Obispo, 125 miles south and on the coast.

Ballard filled up the Plymouth while she locked the Jag, and with long athletic strides, went into the twenty-four-hour Denny's.

He followed her in, took the end stool at the counter, got a coffee there and a coffee, cheeseburger and fries to go. He used the men's room while the coffee cooled, phoned DKA collect to report, and was outside unlocking the Plymouth before she had even paid the cashier. He kicked his tires while the Jag was serviced, then followed her through the southbound freeway entrance ramp.

Flat country, the Salinas Valley, with far hills ghosting against the horizon. Ballard ate his cheeseburger, played the radio, played games in his mind. Her destination. Hopping into bed with her. From what Bart had told him of that porno film . . .

Soledad, the Salinas River glinting under a nearly full moon. King City. San Ardo. The river off to his left, hordes of oil pumps bobbing in the rich wide bottom land. By the time he had followed the Jag through ghostly deserted Camp Roberts, he had switched his mind to Giselle, on the phone all the time with that slick cat from the bank.

He yawned, a real jaw-creaker. He'd handled yesterday's stakeout while Bart had been sneaking over to see Corinne.

Gilmartin. Could Giselle have something going with that son of a bitch? Not that *he* cared, Giselle was just . . .

Ballard slammed on the brakes. The Plymouth shrieked down the highway skew-ass. He felt it trying to go and gave the wheel to the skid and goosed it, shot across the far lane, hit the shoulder in a cloud of dust and drumming of gravel against the inside of the fenders, got it back and picked up speed toward the Jag's twinkling taillights.

His heart was pounding. They weren't kidding with their warning signs. Goddamn deer. At least it had waked him up.

After Atascadero the road started to climb up canyons between high hills which cut off the moonlight. He went by a hoglike semi grunting its way up the long grade. On the far side of La Cuesta Pass the road dropped steadily, so he could see the speeding tracer-bullet of the Jaguar far below. A cut in the hills showed him the lights of San Luis Obispo against the dark sea stretching to the horizon.

They gassed up at different stations near the Madonna Inn, that remarkable California institution with copper urinals and a waterfall that starts up when you take a leak. Ballard front-tailed back to the freeway, the Jag docile behind, then loafed until Wendy had passed him and he could fall in a few cars back. Southern California coastal now, kookieville, palm-readers and weathered beach houses and beat-up station wagons with surfboards strapped to the roofs or sticking out the rear gates.

The highway ducked inland to eat a lot of cross-traffic all the way to Santa Barbara, where it became limited-access again as solid phalanxes of lights showed up on both sides of the throughway. Heavy flanking foliage, the air crisp and clean and laden with chilly sea fog waiting for morning.

Lucky he'd dropped back, or he would have overshot when she whipped into the La Cumbre off-ramp. At State she took a right, Ballard three cars behind. The Jag's left blinker went on for the sprawling Pepper Tree Motel.

Ballard went by, U-ed, came back into the parking area just as she slid out of the Jag in front of the brightly lit office. All very posh, expensive planting, immense roof overhangs, lots of glass and rustic beams of fake redwood.

Chosen at random? Or to an existing registration?

She came out of the glass-walled office, trim and well rounded in her pants suit, drove back around the end of the building and out of sight down a narrow blacktopped drive between the boundary hedge and the two-decked motel block.

Ballard waited, followed, passed the Jag two-thirds of the way along the length of the building. He would have liked her room number, but she was just getting out her suitcase when he went by. Later for that. Now check for Fazzino's Gran Torino and get the layout fixed in his mind.

At the far end of the property, the drive made a left turn along the blank unwindowed rear of the building. No parking there. Then it turned left again, back toward the street along the other side of the hollow rectangle of rooms. Parking there, but no Gran Torino. The drive made a right and then a left again to get around the office, which was built off the main rectangle. Ballard came out between it and the bar-restaurant to the front parking area.

Beautiful. No other way out. Not so beautiful, no Gran Torino.

Eight-thirty. Yawning, tired as hell and hungry. A few minutes later Wendy Austin showed she was hungry too. Dressed now in a miniskirt to display those fantastic legs. He waited until she had entered the restaurant—called the Tree House—before going over to one of the outdoor pay phones and reversing the charges to DKA.

"I thought it'd be Giselle," he said when Kearny himself accepted the call.

"She had an appointment."

Appointment, hell. A date. With Sly-Eyes from the bank? But he was married, a couple of kids. Giselle wouldn't . . .

"Huh?"

"I said, this is my dime."

Ballard reported in crisp sentences.

"And the Gran Torino nowhere around . . ." Kearny was momentarily silent. "Okay. Get what else you can. It sounds like she's headed for either L.A. or the Mex border. You have the number of the agency we use down South in case you need extra men?"

Ballard said he did, and hung up. He opened the phone booth to let in some fresh air while he worked out his approach. Once you started winging it, the words had to come instantly or you blew it. Through the glass walls of the office he could see the check-in girl reaching for the phone to answer his ring.

"Pepper Tree Motel, good evening."

"Yes, my name is Philip Fazzino. Can you tell me if my wife has arrived yet?"

"Just a moment, sir, I'll check."

Ballard wiped his hands, one after the other, down his thighs as he waited. He wished he could be like Kathy Onoda, who never seemed to tense up no matter how elaborate the structure of lies she was erecting.

"I'm terribly sorry, Mr. Fazzino, we show no reservation—"

"Then check and see if my secretary has arrived," he snapped, building anger into his voice that he might need later. "Wendy Austin."

"Miss Austin checked in about forty-five minutes ago, sir."

"Ring her room." She wouldn't be there, of course, since by turning his head he could see her in the restaurant, but . . .

"Sorry, sir, she seems to have stepped out. I could have her paged in the restaurant—"

"What's the room number?"

"I'm sorry, sir, we can't divulge that information on the—"

"Goddammit!" he bellowed in calculated rage. "That goddam room was reserved by *my* goddam company and is being paid for by *my* goddam money, and you have the nerve to tell me—"

"I . . . Yes, sir. Three twenty-one, sir."

He depressed the hook with his left hand but kept talking into the dead instrument for another fifteen seconds. If he could see into the office, she could see out to the lighted phone booth.

In the Tree House he had two cheeseburgers and three half-pints of milk and a piece of cherry pie at the counter while waiting for Wendy Austin to return to her room. Then he hit the phone booth again. It was the first time he had heard Wendy speak. She had a soft, sensual voice. He pictured her undressed for her shower, standing there talking to him. Further erotic fantasies flashed through his mind.

"Room-catering, Miss Austin. What time would you like your breakfast served in the morning, ma'am?"

"Oh! How thoughtful! Ah . . . Eight o'clock, how's that?"

"As you wish, ma'am. And that will be . . ."

"Coffee, grapefruit and toast."

Before returning to his car, Ballard went into the restaurant to order coffee, grapefruit and toast for room 321 at eight o'clock.

He didn't want her to realize in the morning that the call had been a fake. Meanwhile, he knew that she was alone; that Fazzino was not here and not expected; and that she wouldn't be pulling out before eight-thirty or nine.

Now, if the cops didn't spot him sleeping in the car, and push him around a little for not being either rich or retired . . .

They didn't. But it was still a shitty night's sleep.

Sixteen

Going down the far sidewalk with deceptively bouncy strides was a spare red-headed man in a tan topcoat. Heslip grinned to himself, reached over to flick up the lock on the far door of the car. It was 4:58 in the morning.

O'Bannon slid in and pulled the door shut, shivering. He turned his lugubrious, freckle-splotched face toward Heslip. "Cold as a witch's tit."

"And early." Heslip yawned. So Kearny had been forced to bring O'B into it after all. "Where'd he catch up with you?"

"Turkish bath."

Whenever O'B had a fight with Bella about his job or his drinking, he drank. When he drank, he didn't go home. When he didn't go home, he ended up steaming out the booze and sleeping on a rubdown table in a Turkish bath. After a day or two Bella would call Kearny and beg him to find O'B and send him home. The pattern was invariable.

"Any word from Ballard?"

"He's in Santa Barbara," said O'B. "No sign of Fazzino yet."

He opened the door and started to get out again. Heslip checked his watch. "I'll be back at two-thirty, O'B. That all right?"

"Sure. I'm good till then. Nothing's going to happen here anyway."

"L.A. County Courthouse? What the hell is he doing there?" demanded Dan Kearny.

"He's in one of the parking lots outside," Giselle explained patiently. It was 11:33 A.M. "On a pay phone. She's in the courthouse, he stayed with the car."

"Okay, tell him to—"

"What?" Giselle, who had been speaking with the phone still to her ear but with a hand over the mouthpiece, had removed her hand for the monosyllable. "Are you sure? Okay. Call when you can." She hung up and turned to Kearny. "Larry said that Wendy Austin just came out of the courthouse with Fazzino! Larry took off after them . . ."

"Fazzino's car anywhere around?"

"He couldn't spot it in the lot she parked in."

"Mmm." Kearny was looking thoughtful. "Radio O'B to be damned sure that nobody, and I mean *nobody,* gets up those stairs to Chandra's house unless he's three steps behind. Tell Bart the same thing when he comes back on."

"But, Dan, if Larry has Fazzino under surveillance in L.A.—"

"Then Fazzino has a goddamned good alibi in case he's put out a contract on Chandra to somebody up here, you follow me?"

Giselle said into the radio in a tight voice, "KDM 366 Control calling SF-2. Come in, O'B."

Bart Heslip, filled with sudden hatred, lunged across the empty width of bed and fell on the floor. He rolled around amid the twisted blankets until he could get the phone up to his face and snap into it.

It buzzed blandly at him.

He staggered to his feet. The shrilling had continued. His fingers closed around the alarm clock just as it stopped ringing. He stood with the fiendish little machine in his hand, thinking how good it would look bursting against the far wall, strewing its mechanical guts around the bedroom.

With his luck, he'd catch the flywheel in the eye.

He yawned and padded lithely out through the diminutive foyer and into the equally diminutive kitchen, where he shook too much instant coffee into a heavy mug and turned on the hot water. He went back through the bedroom to the tiny bathroom, started more hot water running into the tub. He wished to hell he had a shower.

In the living room he pulled aside the curtain to stare down into Divisadero, careless of the fact that he was nude. They'd have seen it before, or they wouldn't know what it was anyway.

Gray day, even looked like rain. He checked the watch he'd worn to bed. Yeah. Time for a sandwich down on the corner before he took over from O'B. He detoured to the kitchen to run hot tap water into his mug, then into the bathroom sipping at whatever the water and instant had combined to make. It was 1:45 P.M.

At 1:45 the Jaguar once again swung into the Pepper Tree Motel entrance to park a few stalls from where it had been the night before. From across busy State Street, Ballard watched Wendy and Fazzino walk over to the restaurant for lunch. Fazzino not so elegant now, showing his age a little. Suit rumpled, tie askew, dark glasses to shield his eyes, a billed baseball cap to keep the sun off that pretty wavy hair. Ballard really didn't like him.

He saw them seated in a front window booth, then drove several blocks to buy a malt and fries and two Big Macs while the Plymouth was serviced. Thirty-some hours in the same underwear and socks, face stubbled, and now, from eternally sitting in the goddam car, getting constipated.

At 2:30 they came back out. Ballard was parked across the street again. Fazzino started to get in the driver's side, then straightened abruptly and gestured at Wendy across the top of the low-slung car. She objected. Neither of them wanted to drive the long grueling miles back up to San Francisco. Ballard grinned to himself. He was pretty sure who'd win the argument.

Wendy went around the Jag, got into the driver's side with quick angry movements. Ballard grinned some more. Fazzino went around the back of the car with slow steps, yawning, the GIANTS cap pushed forward so he could rub the back of his neck.

Could the son of a bitch have spent the night in *jail?* It would explain his appearance, his obvious exhaustion, Wendy getting him out of the courthouse. Hell, *bailing* him out.

The Jag backed out with a jerk. She snapped it into low, goosed it up the access road and around the back of the building with a yelp of tires Ballard could hear from fifty yards away. She *really* didn't want to drive.

He U-turned to be behind them when they came out. They *should* right-turn toward the freeway on-ramp. He waited. He started to fidget. Jesus, *could* there be another way out, something he'd missed? If . . .

And the Jag emerged from the passageway between the office and the restaurant. Wendy's window was open so the wind could stir her pale hair. Fazzino had put his head back against the seat and had tipped the cap down to shield his eyes. Ballard fell in a few cars behind as they turned toward the freeway entrance.

He hoped the son of a bitch got a stiff neck. Or better yet, constipation.

In San Francisco it was gray and cold. It had started to drizzle. Heslip turned into Greenwich from Stockton, went up the hill past the Chev as he got O'B on the radio.

"Any traffic?"

"Nobody in or out, except the old gal once to water her plants and once to pick up the mail after it was delivered at twelve thirty-one."

That figured, Heslip thought, water your plants and it starts raining. More like water your jungle, seeing what Chandra's yard looked like. He wondered if he'd be grabbing the Caddy tomorrow.

O'B pulled the Chev out and Heslip backed into the slot. The street was slick. First rain, there'd be plenty of ground-up fenders during rush hour. With the wipers off, water sheeted across the windshield. Really coming down now.

Not so bad after all, here in the car instead of out in the rain under some bastard's hood trying to wire it up with cold-clumsy fingers. Nicer, even, than hauling ass all over the state after that blonde like Larry was. But not as nice as being in bed with Corinne. *Nothing* was as nice as that.

He slid lower in the seat and listened to the rain, and thought of Corinne Jones.

*

When 101 rejoined the coastline at Pismo Beach, the sun was close to the ruler-flat horizon where sea joined sky. Ballard would be glad to see it go: it had been hot on the side of his face ever since Santa Barbara. Sunset would be about five o'clock, he figured.

At San Luis, both cars gassed up again. Ballard had a few twitchy minutes when he missed the light trying to get back onto the freeway, and spent several heavy-footed miles picking up the Jag again. They had light to the top of La Cuesta pass, but it went rapidly on the far side with the mass of the coastal hills between them and the dying sun. Ballard had his lights on by the time they passed Camp Roberts.

It was just south of Soledad and just short of six o'clock that he got another scare. He was tooling along the new stretch of freeway, thinking they'd be back in San Francisco by about eight o'clock—and not a damned thing learned in two days of tough tailing—when the Jag veered without warning across the highway and into an off-ramp.

Ballard caught one glimpse of a lone brightly lit gas station with an incongruous rack of promotional chinaware by the phone booth under a big sign, something-something *Free.* Then car and station were lost in the dark behind him as the overpass cut off his view.

He pulled off on the shoulder just beyond the north-bound on-ramp. He got out, stood beside the car with the door open and the motor running, looking back at the over-pass.

Now what the hell did he do? If they just crossed the overpass and went back south, he had lost them, because God knew when the next off-ramp would be. Relax. Car trouble, that was all. A soft tire. Motor overheating. Switching drivers. Having a Coke from the gas station soft-drink machine . . .

Headlights coming down the on-ramp. Ballard was bent over kicking a tire as the car went by. Okay. The Jag. He was into the Plymouth and pulling back onto the otherwise deserted freeway. Maybe close it up a bit: Fazzino's face, a quick pale blur, had been pressed to the window as the gray car had passed.

And then Larry Ballard laughed aloud in the car. He bet the son of a bitch had been using the gas station john. Not constipated after all. Far from it . . .

*

At 6:03 Bart Heslip unclipped his dash mike and said into it, "This is SF-3, go ahead."

"I just talked with Chandra," said Giselle. "She got the bank's final notice this afternoon. She's turning in the car. Would you go up to the house and get the keys from her?"

"10-4."

Heslip got out and hurriedly pulled on his black raincoat. He locked the Plymouth, crossed the street with rain popping off the fabric. Mother supposed to be weatherproofed, but every time he had it dry-cleaned it leaked until he Scotch-guarded it again.

He trotted up the concrete steps and slanting walk between sodden greenery. Kearny's warnings to her at the studio must have sunk in. Which meant once DKA had the car, he could pull the stakeout and go over to Corinne's and . . .

The door drifted open under his knuckles. He felt an odd chill in the gut. He hesitated, then stuck his head in.

"Chandra?"

She didn't answer. He finger-tipped the door wider, stepped into the hall. Silence.

"Chandra?"

Silence. She was in the living room.

Heslip stood in the doorway, surprised at the way his heart was thumping. He looked at his watch. Six-o-six. Cross the room. Use a handkerchief to pick up the phone. Dial 553-0123 with the capped tip of your Bic fine-line.

As he reported it to the police, he made himself look at it. Not much blood. One of the first frenzied blows must have killed her, so the heart had stopped pumping. The rest must have been sheer panic. Or sheer indulgence.

What made him queasy were the fingers, pointing off from the hands in unexpected directions. And the ear. Ripped off by the savagery of the attack, it lay in the middle of the rug a full three yards from the shapeless head.

Seventeen

Ballard stifled a yawn as he drove slowly by 2416 Pacific Street. It was 8:35 P.M. The rain had lessened to a fine mist. The Jaguar was just passing beneath the opening garage door, its reflected headlights silhouetting their heads and gleaming off the dark side of the Gran Torino.

After turning in a driveway down the block, Ballard cut his lights and drifted to the curb across from the house. Fazzino and the girl were just emerging with their suitcases. The door rattled down automatically behind them. Lights sprang up behind the curtained windows less than a minute after they mounted the front steps.

Ballard fought a brief battle with duty, lost, and flipped on the radio to call the office. Probably nobody there this time of night, but at least he ought to make the gesture before going home and getting a shower and falling into bed and . . .

"This is KDM 366 Control." Not Kearny. Giselle. "What's your 10-20, Larry?"

"Pacific and Steiner. What are you doing there?"

That was when she told him about Chandra.

"You're watching the house from two-thirty on," said the Homicide inspector in obvious disbelief. "Nobody in and nobody out, and yet—"

"That's the way it happened," insisted Heslip doggedly.

The interrogation was going on in the kitchen. From down the hall came the white blip of a flash camera before the technicians zipped up what was left of Chandra in a canvas bag.

"Sure. Only at six-o-three you're told she *just* phoned your office. *Just.* At six-o-six you enter the house and find the old lady spread around the front room like somebody dropped the jam jar."

"What were you working on?" asked the other Homicide cop. He was also big, salt-and-pepper to his partner's baldness, but despite that, nearly interchangeable with him. Big men who worked well together because they had worked together for a long time.

"I don't know," said Heslip.

"This is a *homicide,* Heslip. As in Murder One? That I-don't-know shit don't go with us."

"It's all I've got. I was told to come over here and watch the house. Nobody in or out unless I was there. Nobody went in or out."

"She suicided?" demanded the first cop savagely.

A uniformed patrolman came down the hall. Everyone was waiting for some solid facts from the M.E. The kitchen had a white-tiled drainboard and a gas stove with a black stovepipe probably as old as the house.

"Keep talking," yawned the second cop. "I love to hear an educated nigger talk."

"Spell 'educated' for me."

"I don't think I can," said the cop in a surprised voice.

Heslip yawned himself, not a phony one like the cop's. Those all-night stakeouts took it out of you. "Why not call my boss and talk to him?"

"Yeah." The first cop turned to the patrolman. "Yeah?"

"That door at the end of Edith Alley doesn't lead to an apartment at all, Inspector. It leads to a garden, just on the other side of the fence around this yard."

"Yeah!" Both Homicide men were on their feet, almost in unison. The one who'd tried to get Heslip sore to see if he'd spill anything said, "On the front with the back wide open. Beautiful!"

"One of my better days," said Heslip modestly. "Mind if I come along for a look?"

"Come along. We can always shoot if you try to run."

"We'd probably miss him," said the first cop sadly.

*

It was nine in the morning and Kearny's cubbyhole was crowded with too many people. Benny Nicoletti was raging, which had caught Giselle entirely by surprise. She'd taught Benny's daughter to type skip letters and how to handle the complicated DKA phone system, and had always thought of him as a big old teddy bear.

Right now he was more like a grizzly.

"Dammit, Dan, why didn't I know about those hundred-dollar bills until this morning?"

"Tell me what they're evidence of, Benny, and I'll apologize."

"They indicate a payoff—"

"Evidence, Benny."

"Ballard saw Fazzino in and around her car in South Park—"

"Evidence, Benny," repeated Kearny implacably.

"All right, goddammit, no evidence," he admitted darkly, his cold eyes incongruous in his round mild face. "But goddammit, I cooperate with you, knowing damn well that attack on old Ed Dorsey has something to do with mob business, and what happens?"

Kearny looked up from lighting a cigarette. He seemed unperturbed by Nicoletti's outburst. "What happens, Benny?"

Nicoletti swept an arm to indicate Ballard and Heslip, leaning against the filing cabinets behind Kearny's desk in identical poses, arms crossed on their chests.

"An old lady I don't know nothing about gets beat to a goddam pudding in her house with *one* of these clowns camped on her doorstep. And the *other* one furnishes an airtight alibi for the guy most likely to have hit her."

"Or have *had* her hit," amended Kearny. "Any muscle in from outside?"

"Not a whisper," said Nicoletti in a milder voice. "Could be some pro we don't know nothing about, of course, but there's just no word on the street, Dan. None at all."

"What about Garofolo?" asked Heslip suddenly.

Nicoletti shook his head. "Long gone. Jumped bail, his bondsman's eating the thirty-five thou. Who actually took the phone call from the old broad?"

"I did," said Giselle. "Clocked it in at five fifty-nine."

"And talked how long?"

"About two minutes. She said she wanted to turn in the car, she'd gotten the final notice. Would one of our men come and pick up the keys? She'd tell him where the car was parked. Goodbye."

"Say, six-o-two or -three, you get Heslip on the radio. He answers right away?"

"Instantly."

He looked back at Heslip. "You found her at six-o-six?" He nodded to the big inspector. Nicoletti nodded to himself. "So whoever done it had enough time, all right. *Just* enough time."

"To do . . . all that?" asked Giselle faintly.

Nicoletti nodded. He seemed unable to visualize the welter of sodden flesh and pulverized bone that Bart's terse description had made vivid to her. Or maybe violent death no longer had any emotional impact on him.

"It don't take long, lady. The lab is still sorting it out, but they figure something like a cane. That length and diameter, anyway, maybe weighted. Thirty, forty blows. Would take maybe a minute, two minutes even if he stopped to rest."

"Not very professional," said Kearny thoughtfully.

"Yeah. Lots of emotion, looks like. Last ones must of been like whackin' a mud puddle with a stick."

Giselle made a small noise in her throat and stood up quickly. "Anyone for coffee?"

"I gotta get back to Sixth and Bryant," said Nicoletti. "Dan, I expect to get anything you come up with on this. *Anything.*"

Kearny asked almost irritably, "What the hell would that be, Benny? Fazzino was a hundred and fifty miles down the pike when she got it. If he hired it done, you'll come up with it a lot quicker than we ever could."

"Yeah. I expect to get anything you come up with. *Anything.*"

When he was gone, there was silence in the cubicle. Giselle caught herself wondering, and was immediately ashamed of herself for the thought, whether Petie could meet her that night. If only he would tell his wife about them, so . . .

"Bart, what did the Homicide cops turn up in Edith Alley last night?" Kearny asked, breaking her reverie.

"Not much. One old Italian chick saw a couple of spades going down the alley at maybe four o'clock, out at four-twenty. Some young chick coming back from the laundromat on the corner of Greenwich and Grant at five forty-five met an old man with a limp coming out of the alley. It was still misting then, but she sat under cover on her front steps playing with a cat named Red Rooster until six-thirteen. She has the times so exact because she was waiting for her clothes to come out of the dryer. Nobody in or out of the access door at the end of the alley during that half-hour."

The door at the end of Edith, which Kearny had thought went into the building that blocked off the alley, actually led down to a small garden. The building really fronted on Greenwich Street. Directly behind the garden, and separated from it by the fence, was Chandra's yard. Because of the slope of Telegraph Hill, both the garden and Chandra's yard were in effect terraces, so the fence that was only neck-high at the back of the garden was twelve feet high on Chandra's side.

Climb over the fence, drop the dozen feet to Chandra's yard, cross to the back door completely hidden by foliage, go in, do it. Use one of the numerous gnarled old trees to climb back out again. Simple.

Except that it had happened between Chandra's hanging up after her call to Giselle—6:01—and Heslip's entering Chandra's house—6:06. And Heslip had been covering the Greenwich side and the girl in Edith Alley had said no one had gone in through the alley side between 5:45 and 6:13 . . .

Kearny realized that Ballard had asked him a question. "Huh?"

"I was wondering what we do now."

"We dig. Louisa Padilla. Wendy Austin. Who is she? Where did she come from? Who owns Funky Threads? What was Fazzino doing in L.A. . . ."

And what was the significance of the fact that *still* no syndicate troops were showing in this thing? And behind everything, Wayne Hawkley, the smooth old attorney. How much did he know—or not know—about what was going on?

But first, Los Angles. With Larry Ballard.

EIGHTEEN

THE CLERK of Department 2, Municipal Court in and for the County of Los Angles, looked up from his docket book and nodded. He was into his forties and smoked a pipe that smelled like cherry-tree cuttings. A comfortable-looking man, as Kearny had found many pipe-smokers to be.

"Here it is. Fazzino, Philip. Picked up just about midnight on October twenty-ninth . . ."

"Monday night?" asked Kearny.

It was 9:15 on Thursday morning. Last night had been Hallowe'en, and he'd just remembered, the kids had been giving their big party. He'd been on the road with Ballard and had forgotten all about it.

"Monday. That's right, sir. Penal Code 647S."

"Drunk and Disorderly?" demanded Kearny sharply. It was a false note. He didn't see Fazzino letting himself that far out of control.

"Um . . . no, as a matter of fact. Drunk in and around a Vehicle."

"Drunk driving?" asked Ballard.

"He wasn't driving, a cabby was. Fazzino got in a beef with him over the fare. There was a scuffle, officers were called in . . ." He stuck the pipe back between strong yellowish teeth and consulted the docket, then took it out to say, "Bail, three hundred fifty bucks, deposited by a young lady at eleven o'clock Tuesday morning."

"Miss Wendy Austin?"

He nodded to Kearny. "Yes. Pleaded not guilty, hearing is set for later this month."

Ballard was ready to go, figuring they'd got it all here, but Kearny paused over his thank-yous. "Isn't there a bail schedule posted for this sort of misdemeanor?"

"Oh, sure. If he'd had the cash with him . . ."

"Thanks again." They started out, then Kearny made a disgusted face and turned back once again. "Could we have that cabdriver's name and address?" He lowered his voice to a confidential rumble. "Between you and me, our client doesn't remember *anything.*"

The pipe-smoker laughed and gave them the information. Jacob Christie, 1463 Hosmer Lane. The kicker was in the city.

Santa Barbara, California. A *hundred-mile* taxi ride.

The booking sergeant was also in his forties but did not smoke a pipe. He had the face of a man with an ulcer who hates milk.

"No way, sonny," he said to Ballard. Kearny was letting the young detective have this one, but it wasn't working out. "You want to see the Property Receipt Log, you gimme something from a judge."

Ballard could imagine Kearny leaning against the corridor wall outside the room, a cigarette smoldering between his fingers and a wise-ass expression on his face.

"Well, Sergeant, you see . . . Well, Mr. Fazzino felt he had more money than he got back."

"He figures we stole it, huh?" The sergeant thrust an unpleasant face across the desk at Ballard. "A court order, kid. Period."

"Shove it," said Ballard. But he said it under his breath as he left the office.

Kearny unstuck himself from the wall to fall into step with him. Grinning, of course, the son of a bitch. "You really handled that one beautifully, Larry."

"That sour bastard—"

"Mr. Fazzino felt he had more money than you gave back to him," said Kearny in a fair imitation of Ballard's voice. "Why didn't you just call him a thief?"

"Why do we want to see the property list anyway?" demanded Ballard irritably.

"Because Fazzino spent a night in jail." He put out a detaining hand to a pleasant-faced black cop going by with two styrofoam cups of coffee. "Could you direct us to the office of the property custodian?"

It was one floor down, behind a closed door which had a thick glass pane to waist level, with crisscrossed steel wires embedded in the glass.

Kearny paused outside it. "Let me handle this one, Larry."

As Ballard watched, a look of boredom came into Kearny's eyes. His shoulders drooped fractionally, left a little lower than the right as would befit a man who did a lot of thankless paperwork. He dangled an unlit cigarette from one corner of his mouth to soften his rock-hard jaw. His coat hung open. His hand smeared ashes down his lapel.

They pushed through the door. Inside was a narrow stuffy room bisected by a plain wooden counter. A man sat behind the counter in a swivel chair. Behind him the walls were lined with plain wooden bins crammed with possessions. The room smelled vaguely of dirty laundry. The door at the far end had what looked like a good lock on it.

Kearny flopped his license photostat open on the counter while barely stifling a yawn. The man behind the counter looked at it without curiosity; only his uniform suggested he was a cop.

"Yeah?"

"Sergeant Barton said you'd maybe still have the property itemization on Fazzino. Philip Fazzino. Monday, the twenty-ninth."

"I ain't supposed to show the itemizations to just anybody . . ."

"We got a client," said Kearny. He leaned on the counter, and this time his yawn got the better of him. "Fazzino's attorney. He'll spend a buck."

The custodian looked at Kearny quizzically. He was into his sixties, with baby-blue eyes and fine silky white hair. "You're the tiredest man I ever seen," he said. He leaned closer. "Barton really send you down here?"

Kearny grinned sleepily. "Told us to go to hell."

The custodian grinned back and reached under the counter. "He's a pistol, ain't he? Got an ulcer. You say you cover expenses?"

Kearny said he did. The old cop shuffled paper, came up with an itemization form with *Fazzino, Philip* typed across the top. He also dropped a sheet of scratch paper and a pencil on the counter. Kearny copied things down. When he was finished, he gave back the pencil and a green and white crumpled oblong he had previously palmed from his money clip.

Outside, he handed his scrawled list to Ballard. "Anything grab you right off, Larry?"

"Leather wallet, personal papers, BankAmericard, Mastercharge, American Express, Diner's Club . . . He isn't going to run out of credit cards, is he?"

"Keep going."

"Leather folder of keys, handkerchief, pocket comb, car keys with plastic tab, penknife, thirty-six cents in change . . ." His eyes widened abruptly. "Six hundred seventy-eight dollars in paper . . ."

"His bail was three hundred fifty bucks," said Kearny.

"And he had nearly twice that in his pocket. That means—"

"Yeah. He *wanted* to spend the night in jail."

Cabdriver Jacob Christie came through the garage from his Santa Barbara house, a big paunchy man with a huge square head and close-cropped thin gray hair and a very wide mouth that grinned easily. Two fingers were missing from his left hand.

He didn't mind answering questions, hell no. Fazzino? Hell yes, he remembered him. Wanted to go to Los Angeles, Christie made him call the central dispatch office of Santa Barbara Taxi Company and work out a price beforehand.

"He sat in the back seat the whole way. We didn't make much time—he kept wanting to stop for a drink, had me wait outside. Carpinteria. Ventura. Oxnard. Camarillo—"

"You remember the names of the bars in those towns?"

The big man grinned. "Most of 'em, I guess, if I sat down and thought. Hell, I was getting pretty thirsty myself by that time."

The trouble had started after Thousand Oaks. Christie, checking the rear-view mirror, had seen Fazzino drinking straight out of a pint bottle.

"Told him not in *my* cab, I'd lose my license the HP stop us. He didn't like that, clammed up the rest of the way to L.A."

"What kind of booze was it?"

"How the hell would I know?"

"Not the brand," said Kearny.

"Oh. I'd guess vodka. Couldn't smell it, anyways, that's why I didn't catch on any sooner. In L.A. we went off the Hollywood Freeway at Alvarado Street. He was getting nasty by then. Said he wanted out at a little bar on Beverly Boulevard. I says I want my money before you go in, that's when he started to cut up rough."

They'd gotten into a tugging and shoving match by the curb, and Fazzino had fallen down twice. Someone had called the police.

"He take a swing at the cops?"

"Naw, I was handling him pretty easy, even if he had twenty years on me." The big man laughed in reminiscence. He had a huge laugh that seemed to well up out of his hard semisphere of gut. "Used to be Shore Patrol in the Navy, I ain't forgot it all."

The police had wanted him to hang around and give evidence in the morning, and he fully intended to when he hit the street. But then he put his hand in his windbreaker pocket.

"He'd went and stuck a hundred-dollar bill in my pocket. Musta done it when we was hassling, close as I can figure. Well, hell, that covered the charge and then plenty, so I just come back home."

It was worth another ten, Kearny said, if the big cabby would write out a list of all the bars he could remember. It took him only ten minutes.

"One last question," said Kearny. "Where did you pick him up?"

"Big motel down on State Street. The Pepper Tree."

Interstate 280 runs south from San Francisco down the spine of hills which separates the peninsula from the sea, parallel to the Bayshore freeway but several miles west of it. The afternoon was so warm that Giselle was trailing her arm out the open window. The white concrete abutments and roadways had a stark beauty all their own.

"Do you realize, Bart, that I've never been on this freeway before?"

He cast a quick glance at her. "You ought to learn how to drive."

They had just passed Crystal Springs Road off-ramp, between San Bruno and Millbrae. Giselle was leaned back against the seat, her face troubled. To their left, far away and far below them, San Francisco airport stretched slim fingers into the bay from which toy jetliners rose with marionette precision.

Heslip decided to ask it. "What are you going to do about him?"

Giselle gave him a quick, shocked flash of very clear blue eyes. All he gave her was a profile. "Do about whom?"

"Don't shuck me, chile."

"It . . . shows that much?"

"I can hear violins whenever he calls you on the phone."

Giselle's exquisitely honed face was almost haggard; she spoke with a sort of forceful weariness that brought his head around again. He hadn't realized just how badly it had been chewing at her.

"Bart, it's such a *mess!* I . . . when I'm away from him I hate myself for what I'm doing to his wife and kids. For what I'm doing to *him.* But then he touches me . . ." She shivered, and quickly delved in her purse for one of her not-now-so-rare cigarettes. In a few moments the acrid smolder of tobacco stung Heslip's nostrils. "He's asked me to marry him."

Heslip was very carefully watching the road again. Hillside Avenue in Burlingame, almost there. He could tell her some things about Gilmartin he'd uncovered while investigating him, but hell, it never did any good. They didn't believe you until it was too late, then were p.o.'ed at you for telling them.

"He told his wife yet?"

"He's afraid she'll suicide."

Heslip just kept from grunting. Now *there* was a laugh. If the wife knew of Gilmartin's endless shack-ups, she wasn't letting it interfere with her own round of bridge, bowling, her kids, her home . . .

"Next off-ramp," he said.

She stubbed out her just-lit cigarette, turned her mind with obvious relief to the folded-open road map on the seat between them. "Black Mountain Road? That one?"

"Then we double back to Chateau Drive."

"Got it."

It was richly wooded, lush country being eaten away by expensive subdivisions. Chateau dropped them down the face of the ridge, carefully landscaped estates to the right, the Hillsborough Reservoir to the left. Below them were the emerald-green fairways of the Burlingame Country Club.

"Floribunda," he said.

"Okay. Take a left on . . ." Her eyes suddenly widened. "Were going to Padilla's place?"

"His widow's." Heslip pulled abruptly off the street under a wide-spreading walnut tree. Fallen nuts crunched under the car's tires. "Thing is, me and Nucci's chauffeur, old black cat named Jeter, are buddies, and he told me . . ."

Sally Prichard, the Nuccis' housekeeper, had been abruptly fired after hearing parts of an argument between Nucci and Mrs. Louisa Padilla and a slim handsome wavy-haired man Sally had never seen before.

"Fazzino?" asked Giselle tightly.

"The description fits."

And the timing was interesting, too. It was just after Padilla's death, when the transfer of his stock to Fazzino had been proposed. Louisa Padilla had screamed a number of things containing "damned" and "murder" and "evil" at the slim wavy-haired man.

"Of course. They'd need her permission for the transfer, wouldn't they?" Giselle looked over at him keenly. "You going to tell me how you want to play this?"

"You figured I stopped here to put the make on you?"

Dan Kearny and Larry Ballard were at the Tree House, Ballard feeling dejected and Kearny shoveling in a wedge of cherry pie. Every now and then, working a case and forgetting to eat, he got a sudden craving for sweets.

"I would have been surprised if he *had* registered here, Larry." Kearny made his points with the tines of his fork against the rim of the plate. "He doused Bart's tail at eight thirty-seven on Monday morning, right?"

"Right."

"Even if he drove like hell, he couldn't have gotten here much before three on Monday afternoon. Three hours later he calls for a cab to take him to L.A.—so why would he have needed a room? He gets into a brawl with his cabby . . ."

It was Ballard's turn to wave silverware. "Which doesn't make sense, either."

"No? The key is the fact that Christie thought he was drinking vodka because he couldn't smell it. What else can't you smell besides vodka?"

"I don't . . ."

"Water. He didn't even hit Christie—just scuffled with him *before the cops showed up.* Docile when the fuzz arrive, you follow me? They couldn't even give him an alcohol-level test, because he wasn't driving. The clincher is the hundred-dollar bill in Christie's pocket. Christie was paid. The cab company was paid. Everything carefully set up to make sure it was just a minor misdemeanor rap that could at worst net him a fine."

Ballard capitulated with a shrug. "Okay. So?"

So they drove south through the afternoon sunlight, hitting several bars in the stretch to Oxnard—where they quit. At four bars he was remembered, because he had been drinking plain ginger ale in each.

"His first real screw-up," commented Kearny thoughtfully as they emerged from the Neon Jungle. The sun was close to the horizon. "He didn't figure anybody to get this far, so he didn't bother to fake it by buying drinks with booze in them."

"Dammit," said Ballard, "if it was all one big damned charade, *why?* He had to have a reason, he didn't just . . ." He stopped with an odd look on his face.

Kearny nodded at him over the car roof. "You finally got it, huh? Fazzino took the cab to L.A. and faked getting drunk so he could get into a fight and get busted on a misdemeanor. He wanted to get busted because he wanted Wendy Austin to come down and bail him out."

NINETEEN

THE LIVING room was forty feet long and thirty feet wide and sunken three steps below the rest of the house. The carpet was a Bokhara, although neither Heslip nor Giselle knew that. Windows twelve feet high stretched from floor to ceiling, really a row of tall narrow glass doors with wrought-iron handles. Although the sun was low enough to be into the trees, swimming-pool reflections still danced against the glass.

They hadn't found out shit. Heslip was letting it build. The old woman was overweight and fiftyish and dressed in stiff black cloth fifty years out of date.

"I don't know anything about that," she said thickly.

"You said Flip Fazzino was an evil man," persisted Heslip. He was sunk in a soft chair but his hands were empty. They had been offered neither coffee nor a drink. Let it build.

"That was soon after my husband died . . ." She made an excited gesture. She had a heavy Italian face and accent.

"You used the words 'damned' and 'murder' in talking about him."

"Bart," said Giselle, "take it easy. Mrs. Padilla is . . ."

It burst out. Heslip was on his feet. His voice was thick with scorn. "Why are we wasting time with this dried-up old bitch? She knows goddam well her goddam husband was a cheap goddam hood who—"

"Bart!" cried Giselle, her face slack with shock.

The old woman was also on her feet, eyes flashing. "Get out of my house." When neither of them moved, she cried, *"Get out of my house!"*

"I hate the goddam guineas," snarled Heslip. "They come into the black community, screw our women, peddle dope . . . anything for the buck. Look at her!" He jabbed a furious finger at the old woman. "She's got it all now. The house, the business . . ."

"That's *enough!*" Giselle's eyes were flashing.

A very good-looking youngster, about twenty, with very black hair curling down to his shoulders in the current style, appeared at the head of the three marble stairs. He wore skimpy swimming trunks and was dripping water on the floor. His eyes were black, liquid, filled with intense emotion. Heslip gave a coarse laugh.

"So that's the way it is," he said to the old woman.

Her eyes went from him to the boy and back again. She suddenly paled as she caught his implication. *"Madre di Dio,"* she breathed, "you cannot believe . . ."

Giselle cried, "The boy's her *nephew!*" Her face was very white.

Heslip had his back to the side windows. The sun had faded from the pool outside, leaving its surface like lead. His face was nearly in silhouette, congested with blood, the cords of his throat swelling dangerously. "I see. Okay for spooks to screw in the family, but when whitey—"

"Stop it, right now, you ni— Just . . . Leave her alone!"

"Since when do you give me orders, honky?"

"Since right now." Giselle's lips were bloodless, her eyes burned like flames. "Get out of here you . . . you . . ."

The old woman was crying. The boy had backed away from the naked emotion in the room.

The veins stood out on Heslip's temples. "Go ahead, you were going to say it!" he panted. All his attention was on Giselle now. "It almost came out, didn't it?"

"All right, you . . . *nigger!* There! Nigger nigger nig—"

Heslip seized a handful of her heavy blond hair. He jerked her head back, and with his lips drawn back to show pink gums, snarled down into her face. He hurled her sideways against the arm of the chair. At the head of the stairs he checked as if about to strike the slender Italian boy. "You want some of that, wop?"

The boy backed away from the madness in his eyes. Heslip stormed out the heavy oak front door. When he was gone, there was only the sound of the old woman's sobs.

Giselle got wearily to her feet, crossed the room to put a comforting arm around the aged meaty shoulders. She stared dully in the direction the black man had gone. "And they wonder why," she said in a tired voice.

The sun was dying redly behind the clouds ruffled across the edge of the Pacific. Ballard rolled up his window. He scowled into the gathering darkness ahead of their headlights. "So all the way down here she knew I was behind her."

"You couldn't have lost her if you'd wanted."

Ballard drove in silence for a while. "Alibi?" he ventured.

"Has to be. Because he *knew* Chandra was going to get it, and knew he'd be a prime suspect, you follow me?"

"It seems awfully elaborate . . ."

"He's a chess player, they're supposed to have intricate minds, aren't they? Besides, where could he get a more convincing witness than a private eye assigned to him as a tail?"

"I hate the idea of being *used* by that bastard to . . ." Ballard shrugged helplessly. "What do we do now?"

"Find out where he left his car. Since he rode back up with Wendy Austin in the Jag, the Ford ought to still—"

"Hell, Dan, the Gran Torino? It's in the garage up at Pacific Street. I saw it there on Tuesday night when—"

"Goddamn!" exclaimed Kearny. He started to throw his cigarette out the side-vent window, remembered they were in fire country and killed it in the ashtray with a vicious stab. "Dammit, Larry, your report didn't say anything about it. You *sure?*"

Ballard flushed under the implied rebuke. The hell of it was, he *had* forgotten to put it in the report. "I'm sure," he said.

"Okay." Kearny didn't seem inclined to push it any further. "Then it went into that garage a few minutes after he doused Bart's tail."

"That explains why Wendy left the house for the boutique so early that morning," exclaimed Ballard. "To draw the surveillance off so we wouldn't see him putting it in there."

They were approaching the southern outskirts of Santa Barbara again. The radio was faintly beating out country rock. Ballard had to grin. Kearny was happy: he had more digging to do. Find out how Fazzino *had* gotten to Santa Barbara, if he hadn't driven. Check terminals at this end, have Giselle start checking carriers at the other end.

Not that he was wrong, of course. Ballard knew that facts were what broke cases, *every* time. He pulled off at the modest motel Kearny indicated, where the twin-bed tariff was ten bucks a night less than at the Pepper Tree. He went to phone DKA from the room as Kearny signed them in.

When Kearny came into the unit a few minutes later, Ballard was just hanging up the phone, an odd look on his face. "Giselle and Bart are down the peninsula somewhere. Kathy took the instructions."

"So what's bugging you?"

"Kathy said that Pete Gilmartin was waiting there for Giselle." He met Kearny's cool gray eyes. "What's he sucking around for?"

"Giselle's an attractive woman," rumbled Kearny. He was busy removing toilet articles from his attaché case, whistling as he scattered soap and razor and toothpaste across the narrow glass shelf above the sink. Maybe Larry'd come up with a way to shake Giselle loose before DKA got hurt through her confusion over divided loyalties. Or before, he surprised himself by thinking, she herself got badly hurt emotionally.

"Academy Award level," said Heslip modestly.

"You're lucky tomorrow night's my regular hair appointment, or it'd cost you five bucks for a set." Giselle was fussing with her rumpled blond hair in a rear-view mirror tipped to an outrageous angle. They were cruising north through near-darkness and scattered post-rush traffic. She gave the hair a final poke and looked over at Heslip. "That old woman was really broken up, Bart."

"How many junkies got hooked so she could do her crying in an eighteen-room house?"

Watching Heslip straighten the mirror, Giselle realized that he was good, better by far than she had believed. Larry never could have carried off that scene with Mrs. Padilla.

She said, "How did you know that us calling each other names was going to open her up?"

He grinned over at her. They both felt very good, as you always did when you tried something tricky and it worked. "Classical police technique. One interrogator gets so nasty that the other one seems like a friend by comparison."

"I mean the black-white thing."

"When Fazzino wanted to make a payoff to Chandra by leaving money on the seat of her big ol' Cadillac, where'd he choose to do it?"

Giselle started to laugh. "South Park."

"You got it, baby. He figured that nobody'd notice a red Caddy convertible in a black slum area, 'cause everyone *knows* all them spade cats layin' around on welfare drive only Cadillacs. I figured maybe she'd think the same way—in stereotypes."

"I don't blame her," said Giselle. "Next time I baby-sit my cousin's kids, I'm bringing you over to scare them into bed." She shrugged. "The old lady opened up, Bart; the trouble is that her reason for kicking up about Fazzino was purely personal. You're going to laugh when I tell you . . ."

Fazzino had dropped around to the house one Sunday afternoon the previous spring with Wendy Austin in tow. Padilla hadn't been able to keep his eyes off the girl. Reading between the lines, Padilla probably had a weakness for that sort of blonde. Wendy was never back to their house, but a series of telephone calls came. Four of them, Louisa Padilla remembered. She was sure they were from Wendy, and Padilla always told her to get off the line.

"Wendy having an affair with Padilla?" asked Heslip, frowning against the traffic of San Francisco's Ingleside District. They'd just crossed the county line. "Why would she? Fazzino's her style."

"Because Fazzino told her to?"

"And pretended it was behind Fazzino's back? Hey, I like that."

Padilla, each time, would tell his wife he had to go out on business. He would be gone all night. He'd gone through the same rigamarole on the night he was killed. It was a foggy night, his car had missed a turn and gone off the highway and into the Pacific.

Heslip maneuvered the car up and over the long curving ramp which would transfer them to the San Francisco skyway. He drummed the wheel with thoughtful fingers. "She tell any of this to the police?"

"Why would she? Her husband's death was an accident. No, what she was blaming Fazzino for was not keeping control of his woman the way a good Italian man should. She thinks her husband died after just leaving Wendy, and that therefore he was in a state of mortal sin and was damned."

Eternal hellfire for shacking up with a chick? Heslip thought about it. After all the years of strong-arm, dope, prostitution? Hell, you wanted to damn him for something, you'd have to get in line.

"You're right, Giselle," he said. "I'm going to laugh."

Back at DKA they found Gilmartin sitting on the edge of Jane Goldson's desk, swinging an impeccably polished shoe. He was alone in the office. They came in together, laughing.

"Gotcha!" exclaimed Pete. He came erect and grinned whitely and took both her hands in his. He nodded distantly to Heslip. "Out with the sinister black undercover investigator until all hours."

"H . . . hi, Petie," Giselle got out inanely. She felt blood rush to her face almost guiltily. She hadn't thought of Pete for the past two hours. "Wh . . . where's Kathy?"

"A fine greeting. She's in the back office. Some sort of call on some unlisted phone a couple of minutes ago . . ."

Heslip scooped up memos and copies of reports from his *In* box, said easily, "How's it going, Pete?" and to Giselle, "See you in the morning, doll," and was gone.

Gilmartin stared after him with thoughtful eyes. "I . . . didn't know you worked in the field with . . . uh . . . Heslip."

"He thought this one would need a woman's touch," she said lightly. She broke loose, swirled toward the middle office. "Let me check my desk and we'll be off."

Gilmartin sauntered over to stand in the doorway and watch her read Kathy's note on Ballard's call. His lean handsome face was thoughtful. "Uh . . . I guess you've known Heslip for a long time, huh?"

"Ah . . . six years," she said absently. She nodded and laid down the note. "Tomorrow for that."

They went out through the front office and down the hall to the stairs. Giselle didn't stop to say goodnight to Kathy; on tricky skip-tracing calls, the slightest false note—like a door opening in the background—could ruin the illusion you were trying to create.

"You know, Giselle," said Gilmartin as they started down the stairs. "Uh . . . some colored guys . . . uh . . ." He labored to find words. "They . . . uh . . . some of them think that because a white girl is, um, *civil* with them, that she wants . . . she'll let them . . ."

Giselle stopped abruptly on the stairs. *"Bart?"* She started to laugh. "Petie, don't be silly! Bart is a *friend!"*

"A *black* friend," amended Gilmartin. "There's a difference."

When they had gone, the door of the rear office opened and Bart Heslip stuck his head out and stared thoughtfully after them.

TWENTY

THE NEXT morning Dan Kearny had an idea. A hell of a good one, as it turned out, but he didn't get it until they stopped for coffee at the Tree House a few minutes before ten o'clock. Then he sat up straight in the booth, said, "I'll be a son of a bitch," and started asking Ballard questions.

By that time they had been to the train station and the bus station. They had been to Yellow Cab and Santa Barbara Taxi Company and Goleta Cab and Courtesy Cab and . . .

And nothing.

Nobody named Fazzino had called a cab any time on that Monday. Nobody of his description was remembered anywhere. That was when they stopped for midmorning coffee.

"Of course, we haven't checked the cab companies in Goleta, and we haven't checked out at the airport," Kearny pointed out.

The man was indefatigable. Ballard was already getting glassy-eyed. "What do we do after we find out nobody in Goleta remembers him?"

"Then we start back up to the city," said Kearny cheerfully. "We follow your route exactly, checking out every place they stopped, even for a second . . ." That was when he paused and sat up straighter and said, "I'll be a son of a bitch." Then he added, "Describe Fazzino getting into his car and driving it away."

Ballard leaned back in his seat, puzzled. "Christ, Dan, he just . . . Everything he did? Exactly?"

"That's right."

"He'd walk up to the driver's side, open the door—"

"You mean he never locked the car."

"Oh. Okay, he'd take his keys out of his pocket, unlock—"

"Which keys?"

Ballard looked at him as if he were nuts, then, in painfully simple and precise English, said, "The keys for the Gran Torino, Dan. He would remove his leather key case from his pocket, and unzip the leather key case, and from the other keys in the leather key case he would separate the ignition key for the Gran Torino and he would—"

Kearny triumphantly slapped a sheet of paper open on the table, loudly enough to turn heads. It was Fazzino's personal-property list. "Item seven."

"That's . . ." Ballard looked up quickly. "Car keys with plastic tab."

"Yeah. Such as are given out by rental-car agencies. Now, they *could* have been spare keys for the Jaguar, but the odds are he'd carry those in his leather key folder also. He left the Gran Torino in San Francisco and drove down in a U-drive."

"And we've got Giselle wasting time checking airlines."

Kearny was already sliding out of the booth. "We still aren't *sure.* Let's check the U-drive agencies for cars *turned in* on the afternoon of the twenty-ninth."

When they went out to the car, he wasted another five minutes making Ballard describe exactly what Fazzino and Wendy had done when they left the Tree House that Tuesday afternoon. Ballard figured it was going to be a hell of a long drive up to San Francisco at this rate.

Because she didn't want her friends to know she worked a straight job, the girl got off the bus wearing tattered jeans and a see-through blouse—a little soiled around the cuffs and neck—that made it obvious she wore no bra. No shoes, either. A leather vest with three hand-rolled Zig-Zags tucked in the shallow pocket. They contained only tobacco, in case some zealous pig wanted a cheap drug bust off her, but they were groovy for blowing minds.

She was just in panties and putting on her workaday bra when Heslip came through the door of the boutique.

"We aren't open until ten," she snapped.

Being modest about your body was mere Establishment hypocrisy, but they weren't supposed to *stare,* for Chrissake. And you *couldn't* put a spade down for being uncool; spades had been oppressed, they didn't know any better.

"Last Monday I saw Wendy in here at eight-thirty."

"No way, man," she said disdainfully.

She straightened and tugged and adjusted and was part of the straight world in a suede mini and a $50 Pucci original print and square-toed La Piuma shoes. She didn't know it, but Heslip had seen that metamorphosis from grub to butterfly twice before and knew she lived in a commune out in the Haight.

"Wendy wouldn't be caught dead in here before ten o'clock."

As if to make a liar of her, the door from the storeroom was bumped open by Wendy Austin's elegant rear. She came through it backward, lugging a male mannequin as big as she was and in a shocking state of undress. It was 9:57.

"See?" beamed Heslip. "She was here all the time."

"That goes through to the garage," said the girl. "She wouldn't be caught dead . . ."

Wendy Austin turned, saw Heslip, and went wide-eyed with anger. So she knew him.

He gestured at the clothes dummy. "Somebody castrated him," he said politely.

She hurled the unoffending figure behind the counter and advanced on them, her face stiff with rage—and with something else he recognized but was surprised to see in those glacial blue eyes. Terror. Blind terror.

"What's this black bastard doing in my store?" she demanded of the open-mouthed salesgirl.

"Buying a nightie. I'm *divine* in red."

"Get out, jig."

"You used to like us when you were making movies, Wendy-baby."

He shut the door gently on her shocked silence, and swung down the arcade to Union Street. Too bad she'd come in early enough to catch him trying to get a line on her 8:30-morning, but he'd learned something, seeing the fright in her eyes for just an instant before she'd snapped down the shutters.

Intriguing. Except he didn't have the faintest idea which raw nerve his presence had touched.

As Heslip was being booted from Funky Threads, Giselle was talking on the phone with a Mr. Warren Dotson Oates, who also sold clothes. Rather, tailored and then sold clothes, for men only, at exorbitant prices. Exorbitant to Ms. Leonora Wynters, whom Giselle had chosen to be for this call.

"Eight hundred dollars for a suit?" She didn't have to feign the shock in her voice.

"Not for *a* suit," said Oates in a pained voice. "For *two* suits."

Eleven days before, Fazzino had spent nearly an hour in the Royal Clothiers on Sutter just off Montgomery. The previous Friday he had returned to pick up a bulky flat box. On Monday he had deliberately lost Heslip and had disappeared. Giselle was routinely running it down, just as Heslip was routinely checking up on Wendy's early morning at the boutique.

"That's still four hundred dollars each."

"*Plus* accessories. And Royal suits are not bench-made, Miss Wynters. No cut, make and trim at Royal Clothi—"

"Mizz," said Giselle.

"I beg your pardon?"

"*Mizz* Wynters. Not miss. Mizz. Em-ess, *Mizz.* I am a liberated modern woman, Mr. Oates."

"I see. Anyway, Mr. Fazzino has never questioned our—"

"I am *not* Mr. Fazzino. *I* am—"

"Yes, quite. A liberated modern woman—"

"I was about to say an *auditor.* Hired by the *corporation* to make sure all expenditures are legitimate."

"*Legitimate*?" He had the voice of a man who wore a Guards mustache. "Miss Wynters, to suggest—"

"Mizz. What are the accessories?"

He heaved a long sigh into the phone. "*Mizz* Wynters. Matching shirts, matching ties, specially selected by Mr. Fazzino as to pattern, fabric and color. Identical, of course—"

"Identical?"

"The suits themselves were identical."

Nothing, Giselle thought as she hung up sixty seconds later. So he usually bought one at a time like anyone else, but Oates had pointed out it had been an *especially* fine bolt of cloth, and . . .

No call from Larry and Dan yet, either. No word from Bart.

But . . . Ah! In the morning mail a full retail credit report on Wendy Austin, going back to her first revolving charge account at Sears in 1968. Two months later she had bought a junker, and to finance it, had gotten as cosigner a Mrs. Bridget Shapiro of Columbus Street in El Granada. By the map, the proverbial wide place in the road, a couple-three miles north along the Coast Highway from Half Moon Bay.

With quickening interest she saw that El Granada was also only about five miles from Devil's Slide, where Padilla had gone off the road to his death on the foggy night of Sunday, July 22. If he *had* been meeting Wendy Austin behind Fazzino's back, they'd have needed a place to rendezvous . . .

Later for that. Right now they had what she'd hoped for, somebody from Wendy's past. Nobody of the seventy-odd Austins in the San Francisco phone book had ever heard of Wendy. But Bridget Shapiro on Columbus Street in El Granada had. And yes, there was a listing for a Hiram Shapiro at that address in the San Mateo County book.

Let Larry handle the interview. He was good with women if he didn't have to push them around.

The Santa Barbara airport was actually several miles north of the town, in the Beach Park area of Goleta off Sandspit Road. Still squinting from the brightness outside, they walked into the cool dim interior to find the ground-floor strictly functional, with the cocktail lounge and coffee shop tucked away upstairs.

"We do it here or we don't do it," said Ballard.

They'd been all over Santa Barbara drawing blanks. Airways. Avis. Flightline. National. Nothing anywhere.

Out here were Budget, Hertz and Avis shoulder-to-shoulder in a tiny incestuous office just to the left of the terminal door. The two girls and the man who handled the three desks were drinking coffee in fine camaraderie when Kearny stepped up to the counter.

"On last Monday," he began, "did anyone . . ."

Fifteen minutes later they were on the road north again. Nobody had returned a car at any time on Monday. A Mallory Rickerts had *rented* a station wagon on that day, at 11:23 A.M., and had returned it at about two-thirty the next day. Fazzino had been asleep in the Jaguar somewhere between Goleta and Pismo Beach at the time, but they'd noted Mallory Rickerts' name anyway.

He was from the Bay Area—San Carlos—and he had paid cash for the car rental. In the age of BankAmericard and Mastercharge that was unusual, though certainly not unique, but there had been one other remarkable fact. The cash he had used for a deposit, and later as payment for the rental, had been a crisp new one-hundred-dollar bill.

TWENTY-ONE

REPORTS LITTERED Kearny's desk in numbers to challenge the butts in his ashtray. And right now Ballard was down the peninsula, Heslip was downtown and Giselle was upstairs on the phone, amassing more facts which would pile more reports on his desk.

He entered them with the same sense of adventure that a furniture salesman from Peoria would feel on entering his first topless and bottomless bar. After the third cigarette was ground out in his ear by a drunk and the third drink poured into his lap by a topless waitress getting her butt pinched, the furniture salesman might be disenchanted with the Broadway night-life scene. But Kearny never got his fill of reports.

Reports, even crummy reports by field agents who couldn't have found out what happened to the toilet paper in the rest rooms, held an endless fascination for him. Hidden, even in those, would be strands which, wound together, would hang the poor dumb bastard you were after. And these were superb reports, written by three investigators who knew how to dig and how to tell you what they had found out.

Take Heslip at Wendy's Funky Threads. He goes in trying to learn why Wendy went to work early on October 29, not knowing Ballard had figured out she wanted to draw the surveillance from the house. Because Wendy comes in lugging a display dummy and spots him there, they learn she's scared about *something*.

Eventually they'd find out what.

Look at Giselle's work on timetables to Santa Barbara. The only Greyhound from San Francisco getting to Santa Barbara before

6:00 P.M. was the 8:30 A.M. bus. Seven minutes too early. Fazzino had ditched the tail at 8:37. Trailways didn't run to Santa Barbara, and Amtrak's single daily train took eight hours and left at 8:15 A.M. If their assumption that he'd driven down in a rental car proved wrong, she'd already eliminated everything but the airlines.

Valley Air had two possibles: a 3:30 San Jose flight and a 3:00 Oakland flight. Air West had one daily, from San Francisco at 1:15 P.M. Another possible. The best of the lot was the United 9:25 flight from San Francisco.

The buzz of his intercom brought his thoughtful gray eyes down from the ceiling. He saw that his cigarette had burned itself down unsmoked, so he shook another from his pack as he picked up. Giselle.

"Dan, something just occurred to me. You need a valid California driver's license to rent a U-drive car. Fazzino wouldn't use his own. Maybe he could get a forged license pretty easily, but what if he would be in an accident? Wouldn't a little checking show that it was a phony?"

"I'll be damned. That's right, Giselle." He paused to fire up the cigarette. "And unless I'm wrong, that's a felony in this state. I doubt if our boy with the genius IQ would chance that."

"Take somebody with him as a driver?" she asked dubiously.

"Why would he go through all that when he could just catch a plane down? Giselle, get hot on the passenger lists for those flights that are possibles."

"Will do."

Were they wrong about the plastic-tabbed car keys? Well, time—and investigation—would tell.

He went back to the reports. Great job by Heslip on the Widow Padilla. He remembered his cigarette, got in a couple of puffs and started chuckling. Padilla damned for adultery with Wendy Austin? How many men hit for the Mafia? How many crushed with his phony trucking scheme? How many girls screwed casually down through the years, like washing his hands? How many more girls pandered to how many civil servants he'd wanted to bribe or discredit?

Good point, to check with the California Highway Patrol on the car wreck that had killed Padilla. The CHP knew its stuff; still, such accidents were among the easiest to fake.

Kearny leaned back in his chair and rubbed his eyes. He wondered what Ballard was finding down in El Granada.

Her sister.

The same pale sheen of hair, the same long smooth legs left bare by the scantiest of hotpants. Older, thicker, Bridget Shapiro, with a bold nose just very slightly hooked that gave her face a predatory cast Wendy's escaped. The same piercing eyes—without the hardness. Seven or eight years older than Wendy.

"Can I help you?"

"I . . ."

A child, perhaps four, appeared beside her to lay a hand on her mother's bare brown thigh. She was eating bread and jam. Child and mother each wore garish red polish on the nails of their bare toes.

"I'm looking for your sister, Wendy."

"Mmm. Friend of hers?"

Ballard had walked up to the door of the weather-beaten frame bungalow knowing only that Bridget Shapiro had cosigned an auto note for Wendy back in 1968, probably when the girl had turned sixteen and could get a license. Girls like Wendy, girls in a hurry for everything they could get, would have stuck their cosigner for the payments. A flash of ID, *I'm a detective* . . .

But because this was the sister, Ballard tried a different tack. He was suddenly flustered, shuffling. "Yes, ah, do you . . . I . . . ah, you knew she used to make . . . ah . . ."

"Pornies. Sure." The bold-eyed woman laughed abruptly, a good hearty, honest, three-drinks-in-the-middle-of-the-morning laugh. "C'mon in."

He followed her into the living room. Tract house, *Reader's Digest* condensed books and a set of encyclopedias filling the built-in bookshelf, furniture by the room from Levitz.

She pointed at the couch. "Drink?"

Would it help to open her up? The room was cool and dim, the child's bread and jam had left a smear of strawberry on the tanned flesh of Mommy's thigh. A lot of woman, Mommy.

"Sure. Vodka if you have it."

"With?"

"Tonic?"

She nodded and disappeared through the far doorway, daughter in tow. Ballard listened to the rattle of ice cubes. Minutes passed. She came in alone with two drinks.

"Time for her nap." She sat down beside him, leaned forward far enough to click glasses with him and show the ripe curves of unbrassiered breasts down the front of her sleeveless scoop-necked blouse. "Cheers."

They drank. Her laugh this time had subtle undertones. She could handle the booze, probably a lot better than he could.

"You were in one of those pornies with Wendy, weren't you?"

"I . . . ah . . . Well, two, actually, and I've been away and . . ." Something dark moved behind the blue eyes. Bridget Shapiro raised her drink to look into it intently, as if trying to see through the ice-laden whiskey to some reality hidden from him. "She was good, huh?"

"Good?"

"You need another."

She drained hers, making Ballard follow suit. Ten o'clock in the goddamned morning, O'B should have had this assignment. She was back in the kitchen. More ice. Gurgle of things into glasses. So *damned* much like her sister, without the formica surface. Sharp erotic fantasies from following Wendy now being transferred to Bridget. Dangerous. *Mrs.* Bridget.

"A good screw," she said from the doorway.

Her answer to her own question of a couple of minutes before spoke so directly to Ballard's fantasies that he didn't have to fake the blush this time.

She came into the room thoughtfully. "Even under the lights with a camera crew watching? And he comes back three years later? The girl must have something."

She spoke more to herself than to him. She handed him his drink with sudden decision, and drained hers in one long draught. "Drink it," she ordered harshly.

He drank. "Ah . . . your . . . What about . . . ah . . . Mr. Shapiro?"

"There isn't any Mr. Shapiro any more. Not for me. He sends me money every month, but—" She broke off to demand furiously, "You think I'm going to bed with you, is that it?"

"No, I—I didn't mean—"

She dropped her glass on the floor and leaned down, still standing, to push her face against his, hard. Her teeth grated against his, her tongue found his. Ballard got his drink put down on the end table and got to his feet without either of them breaking the contact. They went down the hall together toward the bedroom without another word, hand in hand, like Jack and Jill going up the hill.

What they found at the top wasn't a pail of water.

TWENTY-TWO

WHAT HESLIP found was a real surprise. After Giselle hung up she went down to Kearny's office to see if he could fit it into the ramshackle theoretical structure they were erecting. She figured it had to be significant, she just couldn't see how.

"Dan, I've had Bart at the public library all morning, checking the *Chronicle* and *Examiner* files for anything that looked significant which might have happened in the month or so before Chandra came up with the five thousand. And . . ."

"Good thinking." He waved her to the client's chair. "How're you getting along with Pete?"

"I don't know," she said, the telltale crimson mounting her cheeks again.

She *didn't* know. Last night had been as always, physically, and yet . . . not as always. And Petie couldn't see her tonight, and he *still* hadn't told his wife, and dammit, was he just stringing her along? Oh Christ, what was the matter with her? She was sick with guilt, that was what was the matter.

Kearny was looking at her. When she met his eyes, he said blandly, "What did Bart come up with?"

Back to work, then. Thank God. Fixing her face to come to the office this morning, she'd suddenly burst out crying.

"Fazzino is married," she said. "He filed for divorce from a Constanza Fazzino on May seventh, irreconcilable differences—the usual. I don't know what significance it has, but—"

"May. Chandra got her money in July..." Kearny frowned and shook out cigarettes for both of them. "Doesn't look like there could be much connection, but . . . Listen, have Pete find out when Nucci signed the contract on that Jaguar, Giselle."

"Talk about no connection—"

"Just a hunch. I have an idea that little Wendy-baby gets well paid before she does any cooperating, even with Flip Fazzino. Goods or services. Meanwhile, Padilla's death is still our best bet—hell, our *only* bet—for what Chandra had on Fazzino. Who do we know who'll get us copies of the Highway Patrol investigation?"

Giselle thought, tapping the end of her ballpoint pen on the side of the desk. "How about Mrs. Noesting in DMV? She's always been..."

"I've always been jealous of her."

Bridget Shapiro was up on one elbow in the bed. She ran a finger down Ballard's bare chest. He had never experienced anything like the past hour. Not ever.

She touched the bridge of her own nose. "It started with this. In high school all I could think about was getting it fixed, but plastic surgeons cost money and Mom and Dad didn't have any. Not enough, not then. Wendy's nose used to be like this, too."

He could see it coming, but said, "And now it isn't. So?"

"So the folks paid for it, for her but not for me. I've never been able to forget that." Her eyes studied his face in a bedroom made dim by lowered shades. Her firm, heavy body was deeply tanned, so her breasts stood out whitely. "You were never in a porny flick with her, were you?"

Ballard met her eyes. He couldn't get the easy lie past his teeth. Not after the past hour. "No."

"Do you even know her?"

"I've seen her. Followed her." Suddenly he couldn't meet her eyes any longer. He laid back and looked at the ceiling. "For thirty-six hours straight I followed her. I'm a detective."

"I see." Her voice was very soft, almost humble. "So when a hook-nosed substitute dragged you off to bed—"

Oh Christ, thought Ballard. "Come here," he said in an emotion-roughened voice. He didn't know what else to do for her.

"No."

It was strictly verbal, demand and rejection. Neither of them had moved. They lay a yard apart in the king-sized bed, covered from the waists down by a flowered yellow sheet.

"She's . . . made out of plastic," said Ballard.

Bridget's eyes suddenly filled. She dipped her head. "Thank you," her muffled voice said against the pillow.

Then she, too, lay back to stare at the ceiling, her hands clasped behind her head. Ballard wanted to put his mouth against her breast, but didn't move. He just lay there, thinking what a goddam fool her husband was.

"You're the first one since I kicked Hiram out," she said. "Almost eight months. I've been drinking too much . . . So lonely, so damned lonely, just me and Kathy. He sends me money each month from San Francisco, enough so I know that he's just barely getting by, living in a residence club . . ."

"He's miserable there and you're miserable here. You should take him back."

"I walked in on them, Hiram and Wendy. He was screwing her on the couch." She said the harsh word harshly, deliberately cutting herself on its sharp edges. "I threw him out. If I'd thrown her out, then, she'd have gone back into Juvenile Authority custody."

"Couldn't your folks . . ."

"Dad died four years ago. Right after Wendy got her nose bobbed." She laughed bitterly. "That's how I measure time, how's that for sick? Mom remarried a year later and moved back East. I was married to Hiram by then, and Wendy was running wild over in Berkeley. Pot and crash pads and those terrible underground films."

"And then she got busted," he supplied.

She nodded. "She left Hiram alone until this year. Then she . . . went to work on him. I found them on the couch in March, just two months before her probation was finished. She moved out in

May. Two months, she couldn't leave him alone. She had to . . . to prove to me that she could take him away from me. Two lousy little months . . ."

Her voice was rising. Ballard laid a palm over her mouth to calm her. She kissed his hand. It made him feel like a hunk of shit. "Have you seen her since?"

"Four times. Each time, she wanted the house to meet some *other* man." The bitterness was in her voice again. "They used my bed. I always changed the sheets afterward."

"You remember the dates? Ever see the guy?"

"No, I took Kathy to the movies. The dates . . ." She looked over at him and laughed softly. "Suddenly you're working again, aren't you?"

He shrugged. "It's what I do."

"I might be able to figure the dates out." She hesitated. "Wendy's in . . . real trouble, isn't she?"

"Not so far. We have a theory . . ." He paused. "If it would turn out to be right, I still don't know how deeply she . . ."

Bridget shook her head. "Funny, isn't it? I seduced you because I thought she'd had you. Trying to hurt her—as if it would. And yet I've always looked after her, and here I am worrying about her again."

"Bridget," he said suddenly. "Take your husband back. She isn't worth destroying your marriage over."

"I know." Her fingers closed convulsively in his hair to drag him down on her waiting body. "Once more, Larry. Oh God . . ."

It was twice more. It was early afternoon when he left. On the narrow walk he turned and looked back. The front drapes were open, but there was no silhouette at the window to wave goodbye.

In his imagination, the sound of sobbing drowned out her broken little cries of completion. He shivered. He didn't know if he had used or been used. He didn't think he liked himself very much just then. And he didn't really even know why.

"What did you say?" demanded Dan Kearny.

"That you certainly know how to make a girl feel elegant."

"Not you." He pointed to Heslip. "You. Just before that."

"Ah faidg gkat . . ."

Heslip quit trying to talk around half a hot dog and gulped it down, dropping a quarter-size dollop of mustard on his purple print shirt in the process. Giselle was using a plastic spoon to stir ersatz cream into bad coffee in a styrofoam cup. Her hot dog in the paper boat-shaped affair that took the place of even a paper plate was stone-cold.

"Elegant," she said again. "Simply elegant."

"I said that Wendy-baby has found a new dance studio."

"That's what I thought you said."

Kearny had been watching without really watching a red-haired girl in a tight plaid wool suit when Heslip had spoken the first time, using "Wendy" and "dance studio" just when Kearny had been thinking the red-haired girl moved like a dancer, and that had done it.

"Let's move." He was already off the tiny stool, leaving an empty crumpled cigarette pack on the little round formica table. "Let's go to Chandra's and I'll show you how she got the blackmail material."

TWENTY-THREE

DETECTIVES ARE not interested in ultimate truths. They are interested in facts. Because theirs is an antagonist's profession, these facts usually tend to nail some bastard's hide to the wall, but the detective doesn't care whether the subject is a sociopath, or wants his mama, or claims that social deprivation made him burn down that ghetto, baby. The detective is only concerned with proving, say, that on a certain night at a certain hour *this* man pointed *this* gun and made it go bang bang bang.

The odd thing about facts is that they grow geometrically as the investigation progesses. They interrelate, take on a life of their own, breed like rabbits. Facts can blow your mind.

Ballard's mind already was blown by a fact: after three years of knocking on thousands of doors and talking to hundreds of eligible women, he had gotten laid on the job. It had never happened before. Maybe it could have, maybe scores of these women had writhed around on the living-room rug in frustrated passion as soon as he was gone. But he hadn't known about it.

So Bridget Shapiro, that wonderful sad unhappy sister of corrupt vicious little Wendy Austin, had blown Ballard's mind. As a result he was doing a lousy job of interviewing Mrs. Mallory Rickerts. His mind wasn't on it, his heart wasn't in it, and it was a waste of time anyway.

So he almost blew it. He almost just left when she said her husband was at work. But training prevailed.

"Any idea when he might be home, ma'am?"

"Well, that depends . . ."

A handsome woman in her forties, an air about her like a general's daughter married to a bird colonel who'd get his star before retirement or she'd know the reason why.

"Perhaps I could get your husband at the office?"

She laughed. "I'm afraid he isn't in one."

That was all that kept him there. Too nice a house for a blue-collar worker, this big rambling home on curving Wellington Drive in San Carlos. Forty easy, maybe fifty thousand at today's prices. Sure as hell, *some* sort of professional man.

"On the job, then? If I could contact him there . . ."

"Well, if he isn't off on a charter he probably *is* flying a stool at the airport coffee shop."

That old spurt of adrenalin. Charter pilot! Mallory Rickerts, who had rented a Hertz U-drive at the Santa Barbara airport on May 29 with a hundred-dollar bill, was a charter pilot! And where might Mr. Rickerts do his charter piloting from, ma'am?

"Bestway Aviation. At San Carlos airport."

Mr. Yee was built like a judo freak, short and thick, with glasses and glossy hair too black to be entirely convincing at his age. He smiled a lot and laughed a lot, hee-hee-hee-hee, high and twittering, and had lousy English. His breath was nothing to age in the wood, either.

"You go see, yes? You like, yes? Mebbe rent, yes?"

"We . . . can't see it without the key, Mr. Yee . . ."

Mr. Yee nodded and showed his teeth and gave them the key. "You like very much, you see. Very lucky, yes? Hee-hee-hee-hee. Just come empty."

Depressingly empty, Giselle thought as they crossed the wide, now dusty hardwood floor of Chandra's studio. The odor of sweat and tired bodies still clung to the place.

"He seemed all broken up to lose his tenant."

"Mr. Yee is hiding his grief in his inscrutable oriental way," said Heslip.

Kearny, in the lead, pushed aside the dressing-room curtain and kept going, right around the end of the partition from behind which the red-haired girl had emerged nude and wiping her face.

"My guess is he'll double the rent." His voice from behind the partition echoed hollowly but was clearly audible. "Wonder if he shut off the wa—"

There was the abrupt, very brief hiss of a shower and a burst of cursing. Kearny emerged from behind the partition. Water glinted in his graying hair and he was rubbing the wet-darkened arm of his suitcoat with a towel. "Your turn," he said sourly to Giselle.

"I've already had mine, thanks." But she disappeared behind the partition.

Kearny said, "We know that Chandra sometimes bugged out to her house for a half-hour, forty-five minutes, so if she wasn't on the floor somebody could easily assume she'd taken off. We know she cleaned the showers a couple of times a week. And we know that friends sometimes waited for the dancers to get through working out."

Giselle emerged from behind the partition and nodded. "Every word," she said. "But why would he let Wendy keep coming here after Chandra put the bite on him?"

"Probably to make Chandra feel safe until he figured out a way to knock her off," said Kearny. "I figure she was a walking dead woman from the moment she overheard whatever the hell it was—with or without the blackmail. It's that sort of organization."

"I figure Dan's right," said Heslip. "Wendy, who always took her shower at home rather than here, comes in to collect her coat and clothes. Fazzino comes with her. Nobody's in here, they don't know Chandra's in back cleaning the shower, and they're talking about—something."

"And Chandra hears them," said Giselle. "And doesn't say anything until . . ."

"Let's say, until Padilla dies," suggested Kearny. "Maybe, until he does, she doesn't understand what she overheard. But he dies on July twenty-second and she deposits her five thou a week later. That much we know. What it means we're just guessing at. We can't even prove the money actually came from Fazzino."

"But it *fits* so damn well."

"Fitting things together isn't hard fact, Bart. We're assuming that *maybe* Wendy was shacking up with Padilla. We don't know where, how often, whether Fazzino planned it or didn't know about it. Until we get the CHP report, we don't even know the circumstances of Padilla's death."

When they got back to the DKA office, the report was waiting. Lots of facts, none of them helpful.

Frank Padilla left his Hillsborough home at "about 8:00" on the evening of Sunday, July 22, following a "business" phone call. His wife had retired at 10:30, her usual hour.

The extreme coastal fog had gotten so thick that CHP had closed sections of the Coast Highway to traffic at 4:00 A.M. on Monday. The highway was reopened at about 10:00 A.M. At 10:48 A.M. a passing motorist spotted Padilla's Imperial in the surf below Devil's Slide. It was late afternoon before the Pacifica Fire Department rescue squad was able to haul the wreckage to the top of the cliff.

The bruises on Padilla's body were consonant with a car going through a guardrail and down five hundred feet of precipice. The autopsy confirmed death by drowning: lividity in the face and neck; foam in the nostrils and mouth; blueish tinge to the skin; and the water in his lungs was identical in salinity and chemical content with seawater.

Louisa Padilla had no idea where her husband had been, whom he had seen, or what he was doing on the Coast Highway.

Leaving them right back where they had started.

The San Carlos airport was built on bay fill off Holly Street, on the far side of the Bayshore freeway. Ballard parked in the big unattended blacktop lot behind the modernistic airport building. Room for a hundred cars, anyway; now almost deserted. Must get a heavy weekend turnout. Bestway Aviation faced on the tie-down areas and runways, not on the parking lot. Behind the reception counter were jammed two desks, a big radio, and five teenagers all talking at once about driving tests.

"Pardon me," said Ballard.

Nobody stopped talking. Bestway apparently ran a loose ship. He slammed an open hand down on the counter to cut them off like a knife. "Mallory Rickerts?"

"You . . . ah, mean the chief pilot, sir?"

"If his name is Mallory Rickerts."

"He's . . . in the Sky Kitchen, sir."

Just like the wife had said: flying a stool in the coffee shop. Rickerts was a lean, slightly stooped mid-forties redhead with freckles and fine squint-lines at the corners of his eyes. He had a slow friendly grin and took his coffee black but with a lot of sugar.

"Sure, I rented the car. Station wagon. Monday the twenty-ninth, brought it back the next day."

"And paid cash for the rental and deposit?"

"That's right. Why—"

"With a hundred-dollar bill?"

"That's right." A very slightly defensive tone had entered his voice. "Why?"

Ballard smiled reassuringly into his baffled, slightly angered eyes. Hiding something, but it didn't have to concern Flip Fazzino. Didn't see how it could, in fact, since Fazzino had been right in front of Ballard all the way to San Francisco. But still . . .

"You were down there with a charter, sir?"

"That's right." The warm and friendly smile was gone now as if it had never been. "But no more damn questions until—"

"Just one, sir. Did you get the hundred from your charter passenger?"

Curiosity replaced anger. "Cou . . . counterfeit?"

Ballard looked properly caught out, but shook his head. "We aren't at liberty to discuss that, sir."

Then it all came out. During the flight from San Carlos to Santa Barbara on Monday morning, Rickerts' passenger had offered him a hundred dollars above his twenty-five dollars per diem plus expenses if Rickerts would rent a car and then let his fare use it. It was absolutely essential, he told Rickerts, that no one know he was in Santa Barbara. Rickerts had gone along—what the hell, if the old coot smashed up the car or something, Rickerts could just say it had been stolen from his motel parking lot.

He'd taken a cab out to the airport sometime around two o'clock on Tuesday afternoon, the passenger had shown up with the car as arranged, Rickerts had turned it in and had flown him back to San Francisco.

It all fit. Except the fare *couldn't* have been Fazzino. But . . .

"What did he look like?"

"Medium height. Stooped. A doctor, he said he was, in his mid-fifties, I'd guess. Talked in a sort of whisper, told me very matter-of-factly that he'd had an operation for cancer of the larynx. Smoked glasses and a lot of white hair and a slight limp and a cane."

Twenty-Four

"GISELLE, GIVE us those four dates," said Dan Kearny.

Ballard looked up from his coffee quickly. "Which four dates?"

It was Tuesday noon. Kearny had spent the morning with the reports again, then had called the four of them into his basement cubbyhole.

"The four times Wendy used her sister's house to rendezvous with some mysterious man." Giselle was flipping pages in her steno pad. "The sister called this morning. She said they're firm dates, she checked them against her household calendar."

Ballard tried to keep his voice casual. "She . . . leave a message?"

"For you? No. Wednesday, May ninth. Sunday, May twentieth. Sunday, June seventeenth. And Sunday, July twenty-second."

"All Sundays except the first one," mused Kearny. "And the last one the same night Padilla went off Devil's Slide."

"All of the Sundays were the next-to-last of the month," said Heslip. "Why would the first one be on a Wednesday, though?"

"That was two days after Fazzino filed for divorce, Larry." Kearny suddenly frowned. "Giselle, did you get the date that Nucci bought that Jaguar?"

She checked her file. "May eleventh."

"May seventh, Fazzino files for divorce. May ninth, Wendy has her first shack-up at her sister's place. May eleventh, Nucci buys a Jaguar that he pays for but that Wendy drives. Interesting, huh?"

"Wendy doing what Fazzino wants—setting up Padilla—after he'd started divorce proceedings as she demanded? Then Fazzino forcing Nucci to buy her a car . . . If we're right, one sweet little chick."

"Why hasn't Fazzino married her, then, Giselle, if that's what she wants?" asked Ballard.

"His six months for the divorce to become final aren't up yet," said Heslip. "What bugs me is that third-Sunday-of-the-month jazz . . ."

Kearny gave a heavy bark of laughter and started reading. "'Sunday, October twenty-first, two-thirty P.M. Subject drove to San Francisco International Airport . . .'" He looked up. "Your report, Bart."

"Caught a flight to L.A.! Sure, I remember. Third Sunday, too, isn't it? But hell, Dan, I never read the L.A. agency report—"

"He goes down there to play chess," said Kearny. "The club meets at the International Hotel on the next-to-last Sunday of each month. About fifty members. Fazzino's a Master, remember. Has a room booked at the hotel on a standing basis, catches a Monday morning shuttle back."

"Wendy shacking up while he's gone," said Ballard. "It could even have been a legitimate affair."

"Or an elaborate setup worked out by him and Wendy. What we have to do is find some way to establish Padilla as the man she was meeting on those nights."

"Was Fazzino in L.A. on July twenty-second, Dan?" demanded Heslip.

"He reserved the room," said Kearny. "He used it. But no attendance records are kept by the chess club—only who played who, who won or lost. The hotel is five minutes from L.A. International, flights take only an hour. Larry, how far is it from Padilla's house to the Shapiro house?"

"Fifteen miles. Five miles from Bridget's to Devil's Slide."

"Bridget, huh?" said Heslip.

Ballard made a rude gesture.

Heslip got serious. "Easy enough for Fazzino to fly up from L.A. while she's doping Padilla's drink. They drive him to Devil's Slide, send him and the car over the edge, she drives Fazzino to the airport and he flies back. Three hours maximum away from the chess club."

"And we have absolutely no way to prove any of it," said Kearny. "Let's see if we can do any better on Chandra, starting with Mallory Rickerts' mysterious passenger." He made points with a finger on the glass-topped desk. "Dr. Immanuel Sanderson went to Santa Barbara on the right day—Monday, October twenty-ninth. He returned on the right day—Tuesday, October thirtieth. He chartered Bestway's Cessna 182 by phone, made his initial deposit with an untraceable cashier's check, used a phony address and phone number, and had his pilot rent a car for him in Santa Barbara so he didn't have to show any ID."

"He's also white-haired, stooped, limps, has cancer of the larynx and is over fifty years old," said Ballard sourly. "And besides, I was tailing Fazzino in a Jaguar somewhere south of Soledad when Chandra was killed. Remember?"

"Were you?" asked Kearny.

Three heads came up in unison. They knew that tone of voice: it meant they were going to have their noses rubbed in something shortly.

"Let's forget that Larry was tailing the Jaguar and that Fazzino was in it. Let's just look at the Tuesday Chandra died. According to the logbook Rickerts gave Larry a look at, the Cessna left Santa Barbara carrying the man calling himself Dr. Immanuel Sanderson at a little before three o'clock. Set down in San Carlos, actually, at four thirty-seven. Give him forty-five minutes to settle up with Bestway and drive up to San Francisco, and—"

"And you put him into Edith Alley at five-thirty, easily!" exclaimed Giselle.

"Wait a minute!" Heslip was suddenly on his feet. "White hair, middle-aged, smoked glasses, slight limp, cane . . . Hell, that's the description of the old man that girl saw coming out of Edith Alley at five forty-five!"

"Chandra was beaten to death with a cane," said Kearny. "All of the old man's characteristics are easy to fake. A limp. A whispery voice. A shock of white hair. Dark glasses. And his girl friend is an actress, remember, she'd know about make-up . . ."

"But dammit, Dan—"

"We're ignoring the fact that you were tailing him, Larry. I know. Later you can make your objections. What started me thinking is the fact that this guy's a chess player. They like complex problems, and they've all got damned big egos, the really good ones."

They were all watching him intently now, waiting impatiently while he lit a cigarette.

"So I put myself in Fazzino's place. I'm young, ambitious, and I've just been ordered to take out my immediate superior in the Northern California organized-crime setup. Method unspecified, but the boys back East don't want any waves. What about an accident? Do it very cute, so the hierarchy is impressed. For this I need a girl who can set Padilla up. I remember a girl named Wendy Austin from some hardcore porn films. She's greedy, gutsy, ruthless, willing to do anything for what she wants . . ."

Giselle was nodding. "And what she wants is a boutique, to become your wife, to have a fancy car and clothes . . ."

"That's it. The Jag. Funky Threads. Fazzino filing for divorce. Reading between the lines, the wife Constanza probably knows she's married to a very ruthless boy. Divorce is better than a weekend in the bedroom with a goon squad from Vegas. She gives him his divorce. Wendy sets up Padilla by never giving him very much—just once a month at her sister's place when Flip is down in L.A. playing chess. It keeps Padilla panting for more, you follow me? So on July twenty-second he's ripe for his fatal accident."

"Only Chandra has overheard part of it," said Heslip. "She asks for dough. So Flip and Wendy have to start all over with another elaborate scheme to get rid of Chandra."

"And at this point DKA blunders in," said Kearny. "Larry knocks off the car before Chandra can get the money Fazzino left for her to pay for it. Fazzino tries to scare us off with a threat and a beating set up through his tame bank VP. But they rough up the wrong man, and worse, one of them gets arrested and identified. Making waves, just what the big boys back East don't want . . ."

"So he *keeps* trying to run us off, but—"

"That's where you're wrong, Bart. He might not think we're very bright, but he knows we're dogged. So he decides to *use* us. The intricate scheming again. He encourages us to tail him and Wendy, he—"

"*Encourages?* Christ, Dan, he was down here raising hell, warning us off, making himself . . ." He stopped with a sheepish look on his face.

"Yeah. Encouraging us to keep after him. Losing your tail in a way that you'll *know* you're being deliberately lost . . ."

"Sending Wendy down to the boutique earlier than usual so Larry will be damned sure to stick with her when she starts traveling," cut in Giselle.

"Okay," said Ballard impatiently. "According to your reconstruction, he's ready to have Chandra knocked off, so he sets up his alibi through us. I tail the girl to L.A., where she bails him out of jail, they're on the road back together, with me behind them, when Chandra is hit."

"No," said Kearny. "That's where we're being hustled."

"Hustled?"

"The rube who wanders into the pool hall and loses a few games, Giselle. Then the bets get bigger and he hauls out a handmade cue and starts clearing tables. That's Fazzino—making us see what he wanted us to see. Only, I've spent the past week just reading reports in this file, and pretty soon the hustle started to stand out. They have lunch at the Pepper Tree Motel, start to get into the car—and what happens?"

"He wants her to drive and they have an argument," said Ballard.

"No. They give you an argument to watch while the important switch is made: *she ends up driving the car.* Remember, *they knew you were there.* They also knew you would wait out in the street while they drove through the motel, because they knew you would have previously checked it out and made sure there was only one exit. Any good investigator would."

"My God!" breathed Giselle. "Then when the Jag came back out . . ."

"Fazzino was no longer in it. I'd guess he stepped out when the car was behind the blank-walled narrow end of the motel building. I'd also guess the rental car he used to get back out to the airport was parked in one of the end slots—with Dr. Immanuel Sanderson's wig and walking stick in the trunk. He already was wearing the dark glasses . . ."

"Goddammit, Dan, *he was in that car!* I *saw* him, slid down in the seat with his knees up against the dash—"

It was Heslip who caught it first. He slammed his hand on the desk. "*That's* why that bitch was so scared when she walked in on me at

Funky Threads with that mannequin! She'd just brought the goddam thing up from the trunk of her car."

"And the two identical suits with identical shirts and ties—"

"That's right, Giselle. One for Fazzino, one for the mannequin. That's the *real* reason Wendy went down to Funky Threads at eight-thirty on the Monday morning. To pick up the dummy, dress it, and stick it in the trunk of the Jag before anyone was around. I'd guess that the stop south of Soledad was just so Wendy could shift the position of the dummy so it'd be watching Ballard when she went by him again."

"But I tailed the car right up to the door of the house on Pacific Street," objected Ballard. "I was parked across the street when she and Fazzino came out of the garage carrying their suitcases. That was no damned dummy I saw going up the front stairs—"

"Why were they doing that?"

Ballard said sarcastically, "To get out of the rain, Dan."

"Surveillance reports by both you and Bart mention that whenever they drove into the garage they shut the door behind them and went into the house through the inner connecting door. So the only reason they could have for coming out into the drizzle with their suitcases was so you'd see Fazzino."

Heslip, at least, was convinced. "So Fazzino drives to the Santa Barbara airport as Dr. Sanderson, flies to San Carlos, picks up his car, drives to North Beach, kills Chandra, drives home and gets rid of the wig and stick, waits in the garage for Wendy to show up, lets Larry see him, and that's it."

"That's it," said Kearny. "How do you like it?"

Ballard suddenly laughed. "You're forgetting one thing, Dan. If the old man in Edith Alley *was* Fazzino, he still didn't kill Chandra. Because he was seen *leaving* the alley by that girl waiting for her laundry at *five forty-five*. Chandra was still alive to call Giselle at five fifty-nine. Bart found her dead at six-o-six."

"That's our problem." Kearny nodded equably. "Until something happens or we come up with something new, that's it."

"No, it isn't," said Giselle. "We can hand the whole package to Benny Nicoletti."

TWENTY-FIVE

"GISELLE, DO me a favor, will you?" grunted Benny Nicoletti. "Don't do me no more favors."

A week had passed; it was Wednesday and it was raining. It was raining as if it had decided not ever to stop raining. The roof was leaking in the little kitchen behind Giselle's office, so her conversation with the big soft-voiced cop was punctuated with the *splat splat splat* of water into a saucepan.

"You mean the Fazzino case?"

"I mean there ain't no Fazzino case, doll," he said in his patient, high-pitched voice. "We're still working on the Chandra hit, but between you an' me, *everybody's* pended Fazzino."

"But, Benny!" she wailed. "All the information we gave you—"

"Was real pretty. You must of sat up nights working that all out. It's pretty but it ain't police work." He stood up abruptly; his wet raincoat had smeared the papers on the corner of her desk. "If it makes you feel any better, I *like* all them detective novels with masterminds an' tricky plots an' all that. But we can't *move* on this, Giselle—and by us I mean both the SFPD and the San Mateo county sheriff's office."

"You could get search warrants—"

"We can't show no probable cause, Giselle. Sure, that accident *could* of been a setup—but how do you prove it?"

"If someone saw Padilla with her at the sister's house . . ."

"Nobody did. Me and one of the Half Moon Bay cops personally spent two days questioning everyone, I mean *everyone,* on Columbus Street. Nothing. Always at night, always foggy . . ."

"Okay, what about the old man in Edith Alley? If he *was* Fazzino—"

"Now, there's another beauty. There's thirty-nine family units, as our friends down to Social Services would say, in that alley, and we talked to *everybody* in 'em. Twice. That old man was *all* we come up with, and he was fifteen minutes too early to of done any business at Chandra's. Nobody was home in either of those two end flats during anywhere near our time span—"

"So you mean that's *it?* You just . . She threw up her hands. "At least you could give it to the D.A. and see if there's anyone there with a little more imagination . . ."

"I dumped the whole thing in the lap of Paddy O'Dea, one of the assistant D.A.'s, on Monday. He studied it until today."

"And he said?"

"The same thing my lieutenant said when I showed it to him." He shook his head sadly. "You ain't hearing that kind of language out of me, doll."

And the rest of Wednesday was no better.

Kearny, doing three weeks of accumulated billing, which he hated, chewed her head off when she mentioned Chandra. Pete Gilmartin had to baby-sit, since it was his wife's bowling night. He wouldn't be able to see her until Friday evening after work, when he'd pick her up at DKA.

So riding home on the bus over to Oakland, with somebody's umbrella dripping water down her neck, she had a horrible thought pop into her head. What the hell had ever happened to the wife's suicidal tendencies? Which was such a nasty thing to wonder about, she felt worse than ever.

Thursday. Another winner. Still raining, and then old Ed Dorsey ambled in to waste her morning. Finally out of the hospital and home to listen to his wife's instant replay, he was raring to go, old Ed reported. But one look at his eyes told her he'd never be out in the field again. Whatever edge he'd had was gone, poor old bastard. More depression. Please, Friday, come! I need Petie!

Meanwhile, Bart Heslip, whose caseload was building up again and who thus didn't have time to think much of Chandra or

Fazzino, knew something about Friday that Giselle didn't. Garnered from Golden Gate Trust office gossip when he'd been picking up assignments. So he'd been thinking of Giselle and Gilmartin a lot, had finally decided that Friday was the night. Corinne disapproved violently; Kathy Onoda thought it was necessary surgery.

On Thursday night Larry Ballard compromised his principles by taking out Maria Navarro again. He left her place with such an aching groin that he swore off Catholics for all time.

He couldn't sleep, so at four in the morning he drove up to Marin and made a very tricky and quite illegal repo from a private estate in Ross. The bastard took a shot at him—it *sounded* like a shot, anyway—so he got out in such a hurry that he left his company Plymouth parked half a mile down the road.

He came back to get it on Friday morning, and found all four tires ice-picked. A lot of hassling around in the rain, and then on the drive back to the city he realized the son of a bitch had sugared his gas tank, too. That was it for the Plymouth, not worth a motor overhaul with 103,000 very tough miles on her.

He drove a repo home that evening, while Kearny tried to figure out a way to not give him that nice juicy Minnesota Oldsmobile as permanent wheels. He had a hamburger steak over on Judah Street, was home by six-thirty brewing some of his superb coffee to kill the taste while making up reasons why it was necessary to call Bridget Shapiro.

A few minutes before seven the phone rang and it was Bridget's voice. "Mis . . . Mister Ballard?"

Mister? After their hours together . . .

"Bridget! I was just going to call you. I—"

But she was speaking in a low, quick, almost tearful voice. "Oh, Larry, I need . . . Can you come to me, right away?"

"I'm on my way."

"Oh, not to the house," she cut in quickly. "I'm in San Francisco and I . . . I'm frightened . . ."

"*Where,* Bridget?"

"Where Green dead-ends up against Telegraph Hill, there's a red-brick warehouse. Left-hand side. The door will be . . . Oh!" Her mouth was very close to the phone. "Come quickly, Larry! I'm so frightned!"

He didn't own a gun. He settled for an eight-inch Stillson wrench. Out in wind-swept Lincoln Way, driving rain slashed at his face, instantly pasted his blond hair to his forehead, popped glistening from his old black leather jacket. Jesus, what a night!

When he'd run across the gleaming blacktop to the old Chevy, he remembered it had no radio. No way to call Bart in on this. Coax the old bastard into sputtering life, then through the sodden streets to the rain-swept Western Addition.

The financial district was depeopled: few cars moved, fewer pedestrians. It was a cloudburst, gutters overflowing, cars stalled with wet plugs or points. Left into Sansome. Only ten blocks now; he'd left the apartment only fourteen minutes before. Rain beat in the open window at him, cold against his jaw, the goddam heater didn't work and he had to keep the window open so the windshield didn't fog.

Sansome and Broadway. Fuming at the long light, two more blocks. It turned green. Start, slam on brakes, stand on the horn at the bastard running the red from Broadway to the skyway on-ramp.

He swung off Sansome into Green, stopped with his lights illuminating the red-brick face of the warehouse. Small, old, two-storied, probably pre-quake, no sign on it at all. Through the sheeting rain he could see a huge padlock on the double overhead door behind the concrete loading dock.

Peer harder through the rain. Yeah, an access door beside it, could be unlocked. A light fixture over it, old-fashioned metal bracket, but the bulb was either broken or burned out or missing.

So what the hell was he waiting for?

He muttered a curse at himself and reached under the dash for his flashlight. Son of a bitch. It was still in the Plymouth. For luck he checked the glove compartment in case someone had screwed up and left one in there. Nothing, of course.

He cursed again, nervously, then got out of the car and shut the door behind him without slamming it. Tense in the gut. Scared, that was the trouble. Water sliding down the gutter ran into his shoes. A car *swooshed* by on Sansome in a splatter of muddy water.

Otherwise, only the rain. Beyond the warehouse rose the tan shale face of Telegraph Hill.

With the wrench held firmly in his right hand, Ballard climbed the concrete stairs to the metal-edged loading platform. The wind-danced streetlight back on the corner skittered his shadow against the bricks. He turned the knob of the access door and silently pushed.

It swung open on spice-fragrant near-darkness. The streetlight laid its widening wedge of light across the floor and up the sides of stacked cartons with import labels on them. For the first time he wondered what Bridget was doing in a warehouse.

More crates behind the door stopped it from swinging any wider.

"Bridget," he called softly. His voice seemed lost in space.

But she answered almost instantly. "Larry? Oh, thank God!"

He stepped quickly through the doorway. He could see, by the light filtering through the high windows of the immense two-story brick box, that narrow passageways led off between the stacked cardboard crates. To his right was a wide-open space in front of the loading doors.

"Over here," she called. "Beyond the doors."

He saw her silhouette against the stacked cartons. He started toward her.

That's when a dark shape was launched from the catwalk above the double doors, directly onto Larry Ballard's back.

Twenty-Six

PETE GILMARTIN reached across the narrow table to take the raven-haired girl's hand. He conveyed it reverently to his lips. She giggled. She had rich pouty lips and eyes swimming in mascara. Bart Heslip, perched on a bar stool off to one side, noted without interest that her skirt didn't quite cover her panties.

This instead of Giselle?

Gilmartin raised his lips from the pudgy fingers. He gazed into what were probably the eyes in the midst of all that make-up. "To think, Shirlee, you've been with the bank for *weeks* and I didn't notice . . ."

She giggled. "*Oh, Mister* Gilmartin—"

"Call me Petie," he said. "We'll have some more sparkling burgundy and then we can order. The *escargots* are especially fine here . . ."

His eyes shifted beyond her in search of the waiter, and his voice left the sentence hanging. Heslip, sloshing bourbon with a reckless toss of the head and timing his move, caught Gilmartin's eye casually, did an exaggerated double-take, then raised his drink in loose-lipped salute.

Then he turned away. *Had* that bastard.

Gilmartin, impeccable as always except for the artistic curl of dark hair across his forehead, appeared at Heslip's elbow.

Heslip finally realized he was there. "Pete, ol' pal! Don't tell me you do *your* drinkin' here!"

"Only . . . *ah* . . ."

Heslip dug a conspiratorial elbow into the banker's side. "Only when you got a little stuff lined up, you sly dog? Them motels is *soo-o-o* handy . . ."

A tourist trap tucked between two hot-sheet joints in Lombard Street's Motel Row. Old Petie-baby could pick 'em. Beds available at the drop of an innuendo, no chance of running into anyone he knew. Until tonight.

"I'd . . . ah . . . ask you to join us, but you know how it is . . ."

Heslip swung around so his back was to the bar and screwed up his face into a drunken wink. "Yeah, man!" he boomed in a head-turning basso. "Does I ever know how it is!" He roared with laughter and rammed the elbow into Petie's side again. "Wouldn't *think* of intrudin'—though in a way you owes me one, you surely does."

"I . . . don't understand." Petie-baby fidgeted. "Ah . . . I . . ."

Elbow. "*You* know, man! Giselle! Why, fo' you come along, man, mess it up, I was gettin' close to that stuff . . ."

"Giselle and . . . and *you?*"

Barton Heslip, big drunk buck nigger, too insensitive to catch the atavistic horror in the white man's voice.

"Man, Ah figgered she *wanted* it, an' you know how us coons is, cain't never get 'nough . . ."

Gilmartin was staring at him in undisguised fascination. "You . . . you're joking."

Heslip gave his field-nigger-into-Marse Rhett's-liquor-chest chuckle. "Never joke 'bout no nookie, man. I can *smell* a white chick wants black . . ." He broke off and his eyes suddenly popped wide open, so white showed all the way around the pupil. "Hain't fair. There's *you,* got a wife t'home an' G'selle waitin' down to DKA for you to show up 'n' also that stuff over there at the table, an' Ah hain't got none! Big ol' banker type, s'posed to be leadin' one of them exemplary lives, no scandals or nothin' . . ."

Gilmartin's face had suddenly gotten very still. "What do you mean by that?"

"Jes' what Ah said. If them people down there t' the bank was to hear 'bout how you carry on, they'd—"

"Now see here, Heslip, I . . ."

Heslip winked and almost fell off his stool. "Didn't say Ah was gonna tell nobody, did Ah? Jes' said *if* they was to hear . . ."

Gilmartin looked almost angrily over his shoulder at the black-haired girl, who was fidgeting nervously in her chair. He looked back at Heslip, drummed his fingers on the bar. Finally he shrugged to himself. "I *told* her what you were after," he muttered obscurely. Then he turned on his white-toothed, charming grin. "You want a free field with Giselle, friend? You've got it."

Heslip merely blinked drunkenly, slouched there on his stool as Gilmartin turned away toward the phone booth next to the coat-check counter. Heslip lifted a lip unconsciously. Give them what they wanted to believe, they'd believe it—every time. Rough on Giselle, maybe, but better now than after more weeks of ripping her guts out with inappropriate guilt. He wondered what sort of line Gilmartin was giving her before he cut her loose. There was a pretty good chance, he thought, that Giselle might not swallow it.

He set down his almost untouched drink, no trace of unsteadiness in his movements, and padded noiselessly past the gesticulating banker's immaculately clad back and out into the rain.

Larry Ballard felt clutching fingers close around his throat as his attacker's weight bore him to the floor. He tore an arm free in the dark, swung his wrench blindly with all his strength. It connected with a sickening crunch. Sudden terror in his soul, he crouched in the dark beside the motionless body. He'd just crushed a skull. He'd killed a man.

A sudden blaze of light filled the warehouse. With a sardonic laugh, Fazzino stepped off the bottom step of the steel ladder to the catwalk from which the attack had been launched.

"I think you subdued him," he said.

Ballard forced himself to look at the silent figure on the floor. It was a clothes mannequin. The top of its plaster head was smashed in. The clutching fingers, breath in his ear, the weight dragging him to the floor . . .

Imagination.

The girl started laughing nastily.

He whirled toward her. "Wha . . . Where's . . . where's Bridget?"

Wendy Austin stood over him, hands on hips, legs set wide like a girl in a bondage magazine. All she needed was a mask and a whip. Short-skirted dress of black leather, black tight-laced boots which came to her knees. Above them those incredible thighs rose like taut white columns. Her face was lovely and composed.

"You'd like it, wouldn't you?" she asked softly. "That's why you went after my poor old Jew-nosed sister, isn't it? Oh, she called me and told me you'd been around." She leaned toward him. "You banged her, didn't you?" When he didn't say anything, her eyes got suddenly hot and furious. "Didn't you?"

Ballard managed to get to his knees. Poor Bridget, still trying to protect little sister, when all little sister was interested in was putting her down. And where *was* Bridget? And . . .

"Answer me!" yelled the beautiful blonde. "Admit it! That holier-than-thou bitch let you do it, didn't she?"

Without waiting for an answer, she drove the blunt toe of a leather boot into his crotch, hard. He was just coming erect; he gave a strangled yelp and grabbed himself and went down to his knees again. She aimed a second kick at his head, but Fazzino dragged her away, spitting and snarling like a cat, before she could connect.

"Let go of me! I'll make a soprano out of that bastard, I—"

Fazzino's hand cracked against the side of her face like a pistol going off. He said, in a low intense voice, "Goddammit, I went along with this charade against my better judgment . . ."

She was backing away from him, the red print of his hand very clear against her pale features. Her face was murderous. "Lay another hand on me, and . . ."

She stopped there, abruptly. Ballard couldn't see Fazzino's face, but something in his expression had made her mouth go slack with fear.

Fazzino said, pleasantly, "We have a plane to catch."

Ballard, still huddled on the floor, listened to them leave and tried to get back his breath. Jesus, he hurt.

*

But he wasn't ruptured, he decided as he got very carefully out of the Chevy in the rain. Just a sore set of knockers. He started to let himself into the DKA garage, then paused with the key in the lock.

I went along with this charade. Why? Rubbing Ballard's nose in the fact that he'd tailed a goddam clothes mannequin all the way from Santa Barbara to San Francisco while Fazzino was off committing murder? But dammit, that fact made flaunting the dummy a damned dangerous game, didn't it? Fazzino wasn't the sort to let even a girl he was obviously hung up on, like Wendy, talk him into . . .

Ballard finished turning the key and went in.

Probably he'd *had* to go along with the little bitch. She knew it all, could finger him for two killings. Maybe had something laid away in a safe-deposit box somewhere. Or maybe he was so hung up on her that he couldn't bring himself to think of a third killing to make himself safe.

Yet. But Wendy wouldn't be the sort of girl to wear well . . .

In his cubicle, he picked up the phone and dialed Bridget's number in El Granada. Maybe Fazzino'd had no choice, but why in hell had Bridget gone along with phoning him to set him up? *Warn* Wendy, okay, she'd as much as told him she was going to do that. But setting him up with that phone call . . .

"Hello?"

Ballard jerked and hung up the phone in a quick reflex action.

"If a man answers, hang up?"

It was Giselle. Her eyes were red but her pale face was composed. She was massaging her upper arms as if she were cold, leaning against the doorframe and staring at him. Ballard stared back. She'd been right, literally right. But that meant . . . Holy Christ! Of course. He thrust the phone toward her.

"Call for me, Giselle. If a man *does* answer, ask if he's Hiram Shapiro. If he is, *you* hang up."

She did. She asked. She hung up.

"Hiram Shapiro," she said. "What does that mean?"

Ballard hesitated. It *fit* all right, but . . . it was so damned obvious. Why hadn't anyone else—Kearny, for instance-come up with it?

So instead of answering, he said, "Why are you hanging around here at eight o'clock on a Friday night?"

Giselle let out a long sigh. Eventually she'd have to tell him. "Larry, you . . ." She stopped. She plunged ahead. "You know about . . . Pete Gilmartin and me?"

"Guessed."

"I was supposed to meet him here tonight after work. He didn't show up. Half an hour ago he called." She stopped again.

Ballard looked at her. "And?"

"He told me his wife had just tried to commit suicide. He got there just in time . . ."

"Jesus Christ."

"Only I could hear music in the background. Faintly." Anger had entered her voice and her face had gotten a surprised expression as she realized how angry she was. "Maybe it's all the years in a profession where you're lied to all the time—or maybe it's just that . . . I knew. Anyway, after he'd hung up I called his house. His wife answered. I could hear the kids laughing in the background."

"Did you—"

"No." An almost fiercely happy look came over her face. "But I still might, that son of a bitch. I might call back and—"

"That'd hurt her more than him," Ballard said quickly, uneasily. It bothered him to see that sort of cold, calculated anger in Giselle. Against it he said, almost harshly, "Look, forget all that right now. I found out something tonight—"

"And me feeling guilty about that rotten bastard's wife and kids all these weeks!" She snorted and tossed her heavy mane of pale hair. "Go ahead," she snapped.

He told her about the scene in the warehouse, but first explained what he thought was the significance of Hiram Shapiro's being home, obviously reconciled with Bridget. By the time he was halfway through she was listening, intently, and she burst in with the probable meaning of the phone call from Bridget before he even got to it. She even went beyond that, with the sudden ghost of a smile.

"I get the feeling that you and Mrs. Shapiro did a little more than just talk about her sister."

Ballard started to say something, finally just nodded almost morosely, and then said, "To hell with it, let's go get a drink."

"A lot of drinks," said Giselle. "And I won't talk about Gilmartin and you won't talk about Bridget."

Ballard stood up. Very carefully. "I'll talk about Catholics," he said. "I feel like I've been out with one again."

Twenty-Seven

Dan Kearny got the word about phone calls on Saturday afternoon from a rather blear-eyed Giselle, and as a result—surprise, surprise—spent a bad weekend. He should have seen it himself, of course, it was the only logical conclusion, but he hadn't. And now, having had it pointed out to him, he suddenly had the answer to the second thing that had been puzzling him all along.

But Christ, that meant that he could . . .

It was the knowledge of what he could do that kept him awake on Saturday night. He finally got up and paced the bedroom floor, smoking innumerable cigarettes, until his slender black-haired wife, Jeanie, woke up and asked him what was the matter.

"Nothing. Go to sleep," he said absently.

"Is there anything . . ."

He went over and sat on the edge of the bed to pat her hand, still absently. "No. Nothing. Just a business problem. Go to sleep."

Which took care of Saturday and half of Sunday, until the kids banging around woke him up to a headache. By Sunday night he still hadn't made his decision, but he had hold of it: he had decided to decide, if that makes sense.

So he slept well Sunday night, was clear-eyed and clear-minded and ready to convince Giselle that the case was closed when he got to the office on Monday morning. It was very necessary to do that.

"I was going to call Benny with it," she said, "then I thought you'd probably want to do it yourself."

"Nobody calls Benny with it."

"But, Dan—"

"It's just another thing we can't prove," he said heavily. "And even if we could, all they have to do is deny it."

"But—"

"This whole thing is *closed*, Giselle. Absolutely, totally and finally. Got that? Tell the others, *DKA is off the case.* Now, I've got billing to get out and I'm sure you've got some work to do. If you don't, I'll find you some."

But after watching her leave with an angry swing of the hips, Kearny didn't turn to his billing. Instead he lit a cigarette and thought to himself that she'd been like the old, pre-Gilmartin Giselle just then. Well, she'd probably gotten sick of him at last.

"Quit screwing around, Kearny," he said aloud in the silent little cubbyhole. He sighed and stabbed out the cigarette.

He'd read Ballard's report about Friday night, so he called Fazzino's office to find out if he had gotten back from his plane flight. He had, as Kearny had expected. Next, a long-distance call to a toll-free number, where he talked persuasively with a supervisor for ten minutes to get the confirmation he wanted.

Which meant he'd made up his mind. The confirmation wasn't any good for court, as he'd told Giselle, but now he was going to have to act. He'd dug old Chandra too much to let it go. The other one, good riddance, but they shouldn't have killed Chandra. On a practical level, Fazzino shouldn't have indulged Wendy in her little joke on Ballard Friday night. That kick in the crotch was going to cost them.

Fazzino should have remembered that when you play chess with human pieces, they are liable to make some moves of their own.

Next he called a Concord number and asked for another number in the exclusive Piedmont area of the Oakland hills. A number that would be good that night, if necessary.

Finally he just sat in the little cubbyhole, quietly smoking and thinking a number of private thoughts. Taking a step he'd never taken before, on several different levels. But necessary. At five o'clock he opened the middle drawer of his locked filing cabinet, stood staring into it for quite a while before reaching in. Not since he'd been a twenty-two-year-old field agent in Bakersfield.

He waited for dark, reflecting that nobody else at DKA could ever know about it. No one. His decision, solely. His responsibility.

It was dark and it was raining. The falling water took on substance as it passed through the streetlights, so his eyes could follow individual drops until they plunged into darkness. The gutters were full again.

Kearny tossed away his cigarette, stuffed his hands into his raincoat pockets, and walked stolidly out into it. His wagon was parked just about where it had been the evening Ed Dorsey had been attacked. Now the rain had swept the streets clean of people.

Left up Franklin, over the hill and down rich Pacific Heights, the big car drifting easily with the sparse wet-Monday-evening traffic. He was in no hurry. He had as long as it would take. Beyond 2416 Pacific he parked and got out again. Here the arched trees overhead gave the rain a muted sound, as if it were awed to be falling on wealth. He had seen the house often in reports, had a total familiarity with it.

"May I come in?" he asked Wendy Austin politely when she opened the massive oak door. "My name is Dan Kearny."

"Go screw yourself."

He pushed past her into the hallway to stand with his hands in his coat pockets, puddling water on the hardwood parquetry. Her lovely face was as hard as the floor, sullen in repose, as if genuine emotion were a language foreign to it.

"Flip will want to see me," he said.

"A lot of guys lost an ear or the end of a nose for using that name in the old days, Kearny."

Fazzino was in the archway, dressed in slacks and a pastel shirt with a cashmere cardigan over it that would have cost more than Kearny's suit.

"It isn't the old days," he said flatly. "I've got some things to say."

Fazzino made a studiedly weary bow to usher him in.

"Thanks." He added to the girl, who had made no move to take his coat, "No, no, that's all right, I'll keep it. I'm not staying."

"You're goddam right you're not staying," she snapped.

The living room was gorgeous, running the width of the house from above the garage to the far end. Forty feet long, Kearny guessed, at least half that wide. The paintings looked like originals; the furniture was elegant, old-fashioned, period. A few feet inside the door he leaned his backside against the edge of the rather spindly-legged white antiqued table which held the brass French-style telephone.

Fazzino sat down in one of the half-dozen easy chairs scattered around the huge room. The girl sat on the arm. She had truly beautiful legs. Fazzino idly put an arm around her waist.

Kearny looked at them. "I'm blowing the whistle on both of you."

"This is your big speech?"

"Two things bothered me from the beginning. First was Chandra's phone call to Giselle about five minutes before Heslip found her body. It kept you in the clear even after we realized you *weren't* in the Jag that Ballard was tailing, because it came fifteen minutes *after* you were seen leaving the alley in your little-old-man disguise."

Fazzino said lightly, "In case you're wearing some sort of recorder, Kearny, I want to state categorically that I don't know what you're talking about." A yawn lurked just behind his words.

"But then Ballard got the phone call Friday night from *her* sister." Kearny looked at the girl for the first time. Totally cool, so he'd been right about their weekend plane flight. "That, and using the mannequin to rub our noses in the fact we'd come up empty, were both bad mistakes."

Fazzino showed interest. A spark glowed behind the usually flat black eyes. The egoist, the chess player. Not bothered, *interested*—as he might be by a chess gambit he'd never seen before.

"Why was the mannequin a mistake?"

"Because it shows you've seen our file, and the only place you could have done that was in the D.A.'s office. Since you let Wendy have her fun with Ballard on Friday night, that must have been the day you learned there isn't any evidence for the D.A. to take into court."

Fazzino chuckled. "There isn't, is there? I was in a car down south of Soledad when Chandra died. Under oath, your man Ballard would have to testify to that. As for this nonsense about phone calls—"

"Flip! Flip!" said Kearny chidingly. "Didn't you know they record the long-distance numbers called from pay phones?"

He'd finally gotten to the girl. "Phil," she said angrily, "make him leave."

"I like him. He's cute."

And getting cuter, Kearny thought. She said what she thought he was. He said, "No good as evidence, of course, Flip, but a call was placed to DKA at five fifty-nine on the evening of Tuesday, October thirtieth, from a phone booth near a gas station just off the freeway south of Soledad. We also know that it was little Wendy here doing her famous Chandra impression for Giselle. Just as last Friday she did her famous Bridget impression for Ballard."

"As you say," Fazzino drawled, "no good as evidence."

"My people caught on because Bridget reconciled with her husband on Friday. He was home with her that night. She wouldn't have been calling Ballard, not even to set him up for a kick in the balls."

"Phil, make him get to hell out," she said. "He gives me the creeps."

"We should have had it all the time," said Kearny inexorably. "When we first got a line on little Wendy from a porny-film producer, we found out she was a fantastic mimic. You needed that phone call to Giselle. You wanted Chandra's body found at an exact time, a time one of our men would have to swear he was tailing you a hundred fifty miles away. It was your bad luck that a witness in the alley could swear *nobody* could have got in to kill Chandra between her phone call and Heslip finding her. That made Chandra's phone call impossible, since she obviously was killed."

Fazzino sounded genuinely amused. "How could I be so sure that Chandra would accommodatingly wait at home, alone, to be hit? I mean, if I planned all this I would have had to be sure—"

"The final notice from the bank that you arranged. It gave her until Wednesday morning to get her account current. She'd phone you, of course, demand another five hundred bucks or so—and you'd tell her to be home alone all afternoon Tuesday and you'd come in the back way and give it to her." He laughed without mirth. "You did."

The girl was finally on her feet, eyes blazing. "*Throw him out!*" she shrieked at Fazzino.

Kearny just looked at her. "Don't you realize, honey, that sometime he'll have to take you out, too? You're the weak link. You can testify."

Fazzino chuckled and drew the raging girl back down to the arm of his chair. He turned her hand so the glint of gold caught Kearny's eye. "My divorce became final Friday," he said pleasantly. "We flew to Vegas. A simple but moving ceremony. So if there's nothing else . . ."

"There is—just one thing," said Kearny. "The second fact that has bugged me right from the start." He paused. "No soldiers."

The girl laughed as if he had said something funny, a jeering laugh because she didn't understand. Fazzino didn't laugh. He understood. His eyes tightened fractionally. Kearny casually took his butt off the edge of the table.

"What's that supposed to mean?" Fazzino's voice had tightened too.

"No soldiers?" Kearny showed his teeth in a grin that had nothing to do with amusement. "No *regime,* no crew—no heavies, you follow me? Nobody following us around when they should have been crawling all over us."

Fazzino was very good. He almost carried off his blasé pose. Kearny took a casual step to one side so he was beside and to the right of the ornate little table which held the phone. Only a slight hoarseness in Fazzino's voice betrayed him. "I understand it was a *capo* and a soldier who . . . mistakenly roughed up an old man outside your office . . ."

"Thinking he was a debt-welsher. Yeah. That's what Hawkley told me: a routine enforcement job where they got the wrong guy." That had scored. "You didn't know Hawkley and I knew each other? Maybe you *should* have had some soldiers tailing me."

Fazzino didn't answer. He licked his lips nervously.

"But you couldn't risk that, could you, Flip? Not after one of the soldiers you sent after me got busted. I kept thinking, Mafia hit on Padilla, organization hit, even after Hawkley said the Dorsey beating was a simple case of mistaken identity. I *knew* it wasn't. I'd been threatened. Yet Hawkley believed what he told me. So what did that make Padilla? A *private* kill, unauthorized, because you wanted to be West Coast top dog. You couldn't risk using any organization people on Chandra any more than you had on Padilla, because *they thought Padilla really was an accident.* So now—"

"Now what?" demanded Fazzino instantly, although the knowledge already was in his face.

"Now I tell them that it wasn't."

"Phil, what's he talking about?"

"People who don't need the kind of proof a jury does, honey," said Kearny very quietly.

"Look, Kearny, anything you want I can . . . can give you . . ."

"An old lady's life back?" He shook his head. "Final notice, huh, Flip? All the same a banker or a bookkeeper . . ."

His left hand picked up the receiver, laid it beside the phone, and began dialing the Piedmont number he had gotten that afternoon. Fazzino started up from the easy chair in a single clean swift movement.

"I think not," said Kearny.

Fazzino stopped moving. The detective's right hand had come out of his raincoat pocket with the S&W .41 Magnum four-inch he had a permit for but hadn't carried in years. The hammer was back. His face said he'd use the gun if Fazzino made him.

"Look, Kearny, we can work something out." Fazzino's eyes were sick. "Hang up the phone! We don't need this, you and me! We can—"

Kearny said into the phone, "Counselor Hawkley, please." He looked at Fazzino and the girl. His tongue felt clumsy around the words. "Hawkley? Dan Kearny. I've run across some information that might interest your clients back East . . ."

They sat together in the big useless expensive living room—with stunned faces, like people at an accident, listening to Kearny talk. Maybe they could run fast enough and far enough, he thought. He almost hoped they could. But he didn't really believe it.

FILE #10: THE MAIMED AND THE HALT

FILE #10: THE MAIMED AND THE HALT

When I came to work for L.A. Walker Company in 1955, they were already taking Cadillacs away on a sort of regular basis from the retired full-bird Army Colonel I call Colonel Buford Sanders in "The Maimed and the Halt." About once a year, Colonel Sanders would buy a new Caddy, balloon as much of the down-payments as possible, drive it out of the dealer's lot, and not be heard from again. Quite easy to do in that pre-computer age.

In due course we would get the assignment, Vi Ramezzano (Walker's premier skip-tracer, she was deadly) would dig him out of the woodwork, and some field man, usually O'B, would go find the car and snatch it back. If it was in some other state, we would assign it to a local agency. There was very little enmity on either part. It was a series of small skirmishes where both sides knew the rules of engagement. We all loved the game.

Once, Vi, posing as a previous employer with a W-2 to mail Colonel Sanders, called the colonel's brother's wife's parents in Vero Beach, Florida, hoping to con information out of them. But the colonel himself, there on a visit, answered the phone. When she started her pitch, he recognized her voice from previous encounters and said, "Oh, Vi, who do you think you're kidding?"

It was the only time I ever saw her blush.

When we broke away from L.A. Walker to found DKA, we sort of took the colonel with us. He kept grifting Cadillacs, we kept snatching them back. I even grabbed a Caddy or two from him myself. But I never got around to using him in a File Story.

Then at lunch with a couple of insurance investigators, I was told about a guy they had paid $250,000 to on what they were convinced—but couldn't prove—was a fraudulent personal-injury claim. The story about what happened during their last-ditch attempt to prove it was fraud after the money was paid was just too good to pass up.

And I had just the subject to give it to: our Colonel Sanders of Cadillac fame. And his adversary? Well, wily old battle-scarred O'B seemed the perfect field agent to square off against the larcenous colonel.

Let the games begin.

The silver-haired man paused at the head of the wide steps of San Francisco City Hall. He stuck his silver-headed black walking stick under one arm while lighting a thin cheroot. With his ramrod posture and his ascetic face he looked like an old-time riverboat gambler.

Then he started down the steps.

A grimace of pain contorted his features. Only the cane, thumping heavily on each step, kept him from falling. His crabwise downward progress was agonizingly slow; it was like watching a film depicting torture.

"You say *he* drives his own car?" demanded Dan Kearny unbelievingly. Kearny was pushing 50 but didn't look it, a hard-jawed man with a graying mane of hair and a nose bent and flattened by a lifetime of not backing away from trouble.

"Special controls so he can operate everything with the use of only one leg." Meyer Edmunds was pudgy and perspiring, with thinning sandy hair and an insistent cologne. "That man has just finished ripping off Fiduciary Trust Insurance for two-hundred-and-seventy-five thousand bucks. Don't quote me, of course."

"This special car of his—a Cadillac, I suppose?"

Edmunds nodded glumly. "Colonel Sanders always goes first cabin."

"The Colonel Sanders of chicken fame?"

Patrick Michael O'Bannon had thrust his flame-topped head into the crowded cubbyhole office. He pulled the door shut so that outside lights would not dim the moving images on the tacked-up screen.

"Colonel Buford Sanders, USAF Retired," said Kearny.

"Buford Sanders? You mean *my* Colonel Sanders?"

"Now you know why I wanted you in here."

Edmunds rewound the film as O'B sat down. Daniel Kearny Associates (Head Office in San Francisco, Branches Throughout California) seldom drew the VIP of a big insurance company as a possible client; it had to be something unusual if their own investigators couldn't handle it. Meyer Edmunds started the film over again.

"O'B, this is everything our boys have gotten on him over the past two years—since the car accident."

The clips, spliced end to end, showed twenty continuous minutes in the life of Colonel Buford Sanders. Some in black and white, some in color, some of theater excellence, others hand-held from moving cars or through fences, one from over a transom.

In all of them Sanders was doing the same thing. Limping.

"Are you *sure* he's faking it?" asked Kearny dubiously.

"No, I'm not, Dan, and that's the hell of it. I'm the only one who still thinks it's fraud. We've already paid off."

The lights went up. Willowy blonde Giselle Marc had delivered the ice Kearny had called upstairs to clerical for, had collected O'B's wink, and had departed. Drinks were in hand and cigarettes were alight. It was one of the few times, O'B thought, that Kearny's office in the basement of the old Victorian which housed DKA resembled the fictional private-eye's domain.

"Nine Caddys we've repossessed from that man," O'B mused. His seamed, freckle-spattered face blueprinted a middle-aged drinker's life, but next to Kearny he was the best field investigator DKA had. "Nine. Spread out over almost ten years. And this is the first time I've ever seen even a picture of the man."

"We haven't had a new assignment on him in thirty months," said Kearny as he consulted the Colonel's bulging file.

"Since the car accident," Edmunds said.

"We picked up four Caddys in California," said O'Bannon, "two in New York, one in New Orleans, one—no, two—in Florida. He plays games, that man does."

"With all the computerized credit checking there is today, how could he even *buy* nine Cadillacs, one after the other, and—"

"He looks so good on paper that the dealers just never bother to run him through a credit-reporting service," said O'B. "He's retired military, gets a fat government pension, has a hell of an expensive home in Seacliff—"

"Dealers are required by law to get a certain percentage of the sales price," Kearny explained, "but no law says they can't balloon six or seven hundred of that down payment and get it a couple of months after delivery. The Colonel never makes the balloon payment and it usually takes us about six months to drop a rock on the new Caddy. By then the bank's eaten the contract and it's on contingent."

"But you have *always* made recovery," Edmunds persisted.

"What's to recover?" said O'B. "Last one I picked up had tires you could read through, a cracked block, no transmission, and a crankshaft dragging on the ground. The client took a twelve-thousand-dollar bath when we sold it for junk in Tallahassee."

Edmunds sighed and stood up. "Ten days of additional surveillance is all I've been able to gouge out of the head office. After that we close the file—unless you turn up *proof* of fraud."

"Why us?" asked Kearny.

"By now he knows all my people by their first names."

"If he blows his nose, I'll be holding the handkerchief," promised O'Bannon.

DKA seldom got to mount a concentrated surveillance on a single subject, expenses unlimited. O'B brought in two other DKA investigators, Larry Ballard and Bart Heslip. Heslip was a black ex-boxer who found the same excitement in manhunting that the ring had once given him; Ballard was a late-twenties blond man, just under six feet and conditioned like an athlete.

"Remember, gents, even more important than uninterrupted observation is the fact that he *must never know,* must never even *suspect,* that someone's staked out on him. If he's been disciplined enough to never give himself away once during two years—"

"But he's already been paid off," Heslip pointed out.

"That's what we're banking on," O'B said. "But remember, this guy can *smell* a setup. He's gun-shy. I've been after him for ten years."

"Unmarried, I take it?" asked Ballard.

"Widowed seven years ago."

"Why not get a woman next to him and—"

"Four insurance-company baggers tried in the last two years." Baggers are female investigators, who often carry tape-recorders in their handbags. "But part of the basis for the high settlement was his claim that the accident made him impotent. Nothing stirring."

"If we could catch him shacking up—" Heslip shook his head and chuckled. "Man, two years? That takes some sort of cool."

"He's got it," said O'Bannon.

Ballard was thoughtful. "How about—oh, sports? Catch him in a gymnasium? On a weekend hike? Horseback riding?"

"He does go to a gym five times a week—for whirlpool therapy. They haven't caught him taking a weekend anywhere since the accident. Church every Sunday—stands in back because he claims he can't kneel down. Until the accident he didn't go to church at all."

That briefing was on the first morning of surveillance, which was carried out essentially from the garret room of an elegant three-story red brick whose owner owed Edmunds a favor. It was directly across Scenic Way from the subject's distinctive colonial revival with its hipped roof and second-floor Palladian window.

"With a house like that, servants, a gardener—what's the cat on the hustle for?" mused Heslip.

"You've answered your own questions. He *likes* the hustle."

"There he is," said Ballard from the window.

The sandbagged 600mm lens brought Colonel Buford Sanders up close enough, as he laboriously descended his front steps, to count the hairs in his mustache. Click. Click. Click. But O'B knew, even as he took them, that the stills would only support Sanders' claim. He checked his watch and stood up. "Time for his hour with the Jacuzzi bath. See you gents later."

The therapist, Wednesday lunch at the Presidio officers' club, back home. O'B had the daily routine down pat. It was on the return trip, with Sanders' special Caddy two blocks ahead, that O'B became aware of a new element in the equation. On Thursday, when he popped into the office after business hours, he told Kearny about it.

"Edmunds must still have one of his people second-guessing us, Dan. There was a second tail on Sanders for five blocks yesterday afternoon, and this morning a TV repair truck from a company that isn't in the phone book was parked down the street for twenty minutes. Ballard thinks someone was tagging him, too."

Kearny was already at the phone, having Edmunds paged out of the steam room at the Elks Club. In a few minutes he hung up.

"Not Edmunds. But somebody else at Fiduciary must have had a bright idea. Edmunds will check around, make sure the field man gets yanked." He was on his feet. "Let's go get a drink."

"You'll find this hard to believe, but I can't. I'm due to relieve Bart in half an hour."

"His girlfriend's back east visiting her folks—so Bart's got nothing better to do. And this *might* be important. You know how good Larry is with women: well, day before yesterday he spotted that good-looking maid of Sanders drinking at a little bar on Lincoln Way and Twentieth Avenue where Larry hangs around."

They shouldered into their topcoats, then paused at the front of the garage to set the alarms and lock up before going out into the chill September evening. "Coincidence?"

"Can't see it being anything else," said Kearny. "She just likes to drink—with anybody who isn't her husband."

"That covers a lot of ground," said O'B. "And her with two kids at home. Tsk, tsk. We'd better go speak to the girl."

Jacques Daniels' was not a fancy way of speaking about a sour-mash bourbon. It was a bar owned by two partners, one a small lively balding Frenchman from Algeria who had given his first name to the place, the other a pert little blonde named Beverly Daniels. She and Larry Ballard were talking across the bar when O'B and Kearny entered.

The place was warm and cosy and intimate, with mismatched hardwood tables, myriad hanging ferns, and handmade Tiffany-style lamps that cast a soft stained glow across the drinkers. Lying on the bar beside Ballard were two DKA report forms with typing on them. Ballard tapped them with a finger. Kearny scooped them up in passing.

Ballard murmured, apparently to Beverly, "Brunette by the jukebox. Tailed her last night."

The two detectives pulled out chairs on both sides of the generously endowed black-haired girl. She had a long upper lip that showed precise incisors. Those in the lower jaw had a habit of worrying the protruding lip as she talked.

Her voice was sullen. "I'm waiting for someone."

"You weren't yesterday when Frankie Gallaway stopped at your table." Kearny had scanned Ballard's report for a few moments.

"Your name is Rosario Renucci. You've been a maid for four years on Scenic Way." O'Bannon hadn't read Ballard's report, but he could follow Kearny's leads easily enough.

"*Married* name," said Kearny.

"What sort of scam is—" she began.

"Husband is Ermanno Renucci," said O'Bannon.

"Hard-working guy at a foundry on Brannon Street. Hot-tempered but a home-loving sort of person. Salt of the earth."

"If you think you can—"

"Two children, minors, ages four and two." O'B shook his head sadly. "Rosie, Rosie, what are we going to do with you? Ermanno finds out—" He shaped his lips in a *whew* position, shook one hand back and forth as if he'd caught it in a car door. "Comes home sometime, finds those two sweet little kids all alone—"

Her face seemed about to crumble, but she was still in there trying. "You guys don't beat it, I'll call the cops."

"And we'll call Ermanno." Kearny began reading in a low voice from Ballard's report. "Eight fifty-eight p.m., Wednesday, September twenty-ninth, subject met male Caucasian subsequently identified as Frankie Gallaway at Jacques Daniels', a bar at eighteen-forty-nine Lincoln Way."

He raised cold gray eyes to her defiant face, then read again.

"At twelve-o-seven a.m. subject and Gallaway left the bar and proceeded to the residence maintained by Gallaway at the rear of two-nine-eight Parnassus Street. This is a detached cottage reached by a passageway alongside the main building."

"Anybody who says Frankie and I—"

"Subject and Gallaway entered the bedroom at twelve forty-four a.m., switched out the lights at twelve fifty-eight. The lights remained off until two twenty-two a.m. Subject left Gallaway's residence at two forty a.m., after embracing with Gallaway in the open doorway."

She broke, abruptly, with a half-smothered sob.

"Damn you, you got any idea what it's like? The relatives drooling over the kids? Washing clothes? And dishes? And getting them up and off to school and—"

"'Tis far better to have loved and lost than to do thirty pounds of dirty laundry a week," observed O'Bannon.

"Look, what can I offer you not to tell Ermanno—"

"Tell us about your boss," suggested Kearny.

She seemed dazed by the abrupt switch. "My boss?"

"He ever make a pass at you?"

"Have other girls in there?"

"He's faking it, isn't he? The limp?"

"Doesn't limp once the shades are drawn, does he, Rosie?"

"How does he get the girls in and out without being seen?"

"How much extra does he give you to cover for him?"

"C'mon, Rosie. Give, girl. Give."

Ashen-faced and shaken, Rosie gave.

It was five a.m. on Saturday. O'Bannon stifled a vast yawn and shivered despite the car heater. He was on Seacliff Avenue, a block from the subject's house—where, surprise, surprise, he'd found the specially equipped Cadillac street-parked when he'd arrived two hours before. And Colonel Sanders with that spacious three-car garage under the house!

It fit with what Rosie had overheard Sanders saying on the phone while making motel reservations. He'd be leaving the city around five a.m. on Saturday and would be there by midday at the latest. The clandestine nature of the departure, the fact that the motel was six or seven hours away from San Francisco—a probably five-to-seven bet, O'B thought, that a woman was involved.

He stiffened, crushing the paper cup which had contained his third coffee of the day. His rearview mirror had seen a figure moving with the now-familiar crabwise shuffle. He used the radio.

"SF-2 to San F-3. Do you read me, Bart, over?"

"Loud and clear." Heslip was, by prearrangement, in his car a quarter block from the subject's house.

"He's just getting into the Caddy over here on Seacliff."

"He back-doored me! If he's tumbled to the stake—"

"Just being cautious. I've got him now. Out."

"10-4, cat. Good hunting. Over and out."

O'B already had his car in motion, backing and filling as the subject got the Caddy started. O'B was going to try a front tail, the most difficult but also the most difficult to spot. It meant making an educated guess in which direction Sanders would be going. O'B only knew for sure it wouldn't be west—not unless the Caddy came equipped with water wings.

He pulled away ten seconds before Sanders did, took a left into the Presidio off 25th Avenue when he saw Sanders' left blinker go on. That made it easy. Golden Gate Bridge. North.

It was gloriously clear, going to be hot, with the not-yet-risen sun reddening strata of clouds above the Oakland hills before it burst out to make crinkled lead foil of the Bay through the whizzing orange handrails of the bridge. O'B sang with the radio while beating time on the steering wheel. He felt it: this was the day, this was the trip on which he was going to nail Sanders.

And then he almost lost him. Sanders abruptly veered across all four lanes into the old Blackpoint Cut-off which led across the tidal marshes to Vallejo. It took O'B twenty minutes to get turned around, pick him up, pass him, and drop into line an eighth of a mile ahead of him.

Tricky cat. Start out north, then go east. Actually, O'B liked it. Sanders *really* didn't want anyone tagging along.

O'B had assumed it would be northeast from Vallejo on Interstate 80, toward Sacramento, Tahoe, Reno, places like that. But instead it was 680 through Benicia to Concord, then down to turn east on 580 to Livermore, a hot dusty suburban sprawl supported by the nuclear research facility of the University of California.

"With *breakfast*?" exclaimed the dismayed waitress at the diner he'd chosen after Sanders had stopped at a more elaborate restaurant a block farther off the freeway.

"The sun is over the yardarm *somewhere* in this world, me lhove. So I'll be havin' a wee dram o' the Chablis wit' me eggs."

Stopping at Livermore for breakfast meant south on the new Interstate 5, which was unsullied by such namby-pamby things as restaurants, truck stops, gas stations, or roadside cafés. It was a freeway for the traveler in a rush. O'B was content to tag along behind now—Sanders surely would feel he'd shaken any possible tail by this time. Showed how wrong a man could be.

"Looks like it's Bakersfield," mused O'Bannon aloud.

Which again showed how wrong a man could be.

Fifty miles south on Interstate 5, Sanders turned west on California 152. *West?* Up through the Pacheco Pass? What the hell went on?

An hour later, when Sanders turned north on U.S. 101 at Gilroy, O'Bannon knew. Tricky, indeed! The subject had in effect made a giant circle down through the great interior depressed valley which formed the heart of California between the Sierras and the Coast Range. Now he was headed up toward the Bay area again; if he kept going far enough, he'd be back in San Francisco.

He didn't go that far. At San Jose, 50 miles from the city, he cut over to Interstate 280 and left the freeway at Winchester Boulevard—in plenty of time to honor his motel reservation.

*

The Cozee-Up Motel was a U-shaped affair triple-tiered around a fiercely blue swimming pool masked from the street and the skyway by dense shrubbery. A motel designed for assignations. O'Bannon, his wrap-around dark glasses leaving little more than his teeth showing, was delving industriously in the trunk compartment of his Chevy Caprice when Sanders came from Registration in his crabwise shuffle. O'B watched him into the first-floor corner room farthest from the office, then went in himself.

"Something on the first floor," he told the iron-eyed woman behind the desk. "As far from the office as possible."

"The *very* end room was just rented, but—"

"How about the one next to it?"

"The maid hasn't gotten—"

"I'll have a cup of coffee while I wait."

A window booth in the coffee shop gave him an excellent view of the subject's dust-filmed Cadillac. The cups of coffee gave him heartburn in the two hours before the motel's senior-citizen maid had snailed her way in and out of his room. The temperature rose as the sun climbed a cloudless smoggy sky. O'B resisted the siren lure of a liquor store two blocks away; he didn't dare break surveillance that long. What the hell, his room would be air-conditioned. As O'B was fumbling open his door, Sanders emerged from the adjacent one without a glance at the perspiring red-haired man. This gave O'B a chance to see that Sanders' bed was obligingly headed up against the partition between their two rooms.

He watched Sanders take a booth in the coffee shop, then got the necessary equipment from his suitcase. Using a quarter-inch cordless battery-powered drill and a long bit, O'B holed the wainscoting to come out under Sanders' bed. Through this hole he inserted a delicate high-resolution pencil mike, which he patched into a sound-activated Uher recorder. Fortunately the hum of the subject's air conditioner was not loud enough to activate the mike.

Sanders returned half an hour later, looking very drawn as he limped across the heat-softened blacktop. Probably that coffee, O'B thought. But what if the guy really *was* crippled? No, couldn't be. Otherwise, what was he doing in San Jose, a mere 50 miles from the city but arrived at by over 200 circuitous miles? Why back-door his own house at five in the am? Why street-park his car a block away?

O'B put the monitor plug in his ear. He heard the door opening. Bedsprings. A sigh of relief. Phone. Asking for a number. O'B realized he was holding his breath. Would it be to a woman?

"Hello, Cassie? Just got in. That's right. Of *course* I made sure nobody saw me leave. Couldn't have anyone—what? Yes. What I thought, too. All right. Pick you up about six thirty. We'll eat early so nothing interferes with our night together."

Just what they had suspected! Sanders had a little thing going on the side down here in San Jose and had sneaked down to celebrate the end of his long charade with a shack-up in a motel. Well, kiss your two-seven-five thousand goodbye, baby. Say hello to them cold prison walls.

Cold. Shouldn't have thought of that. How good an icy beer would taste! Send out for a six-pack? No. Didn't want to pinpoint the fact that he was staying in his room.

Sanders was now in the shower, but O'B's, incredibly enough, didn't work. The opportunity had passed anyway, as Sanders was finished now. O'B couldn't chance being under the needle spray when the subject might suddenly decide to take off.

Pool, sparkling and inviting a few paces from his door? No. Same problem.

He tried again to make his air conditioner work. On the blink. Sweat was standing on O'B's face. At least he could get some ice. He found a pitcher and carried it down to the ice-making machine beside the office.

The machine was busted.

He drank tepid tapwater from a styrofoam cup—the maid had forgotten to leave any glasses in his room. The water smelled of chemicals and tasted of fluorine. He kept on sweating.

He was rapidly coming to hate the guts of the man in the next room.

Thanks to the overheard phone conversation O'B was pouring sweat onto the sun-hot vinyl seat of his Caprice when Sanders limped out to the Caddy at six fifteen. Cassie, the girl on the phone, turned out to be a stunning blonde who lived in a ticky-tacky house off South Bascom Avenue that she'd probably gotten in a divorce settlement.

They ate supper at a very fancy place on East San Carlos near the San Jose State campus. From across the street it looked like cracked crab cocktails, rare roast beef washed down with a vintage burgundy, and chocolate mousse for dessert. O'B watched them through the restaurant window while choking down a food-chain's Quarter-Pounder made of a glutinous mass of chopped cow and soya meal. He ached for them to get back to the motel.

But they didn't go back to the motel. Instead they went south on Market Street, right out of the congested areas of San Jose into, surprisingly, traffic which got fiercer the farther from the center of town they went. Abruptly O'B realized he was buried in a crush of almost stationary autos with no idea of where the Caddy was. Left turn into Umbarger Road.

Which meant the Santa Clara County fairgrounds.

The traffic turned again, O'B willy-nilly with it. Dirt road now, a boy with a flashlight waving the Caprice into one of countless rows of parked cars. O'B got out. The Caddy was nowhere in sight. If Sanders had chosen this way to lose any possible tail, he'd sure succeeded. All O'B could do now was hope that the subject and his blonde had been headed wherever everybody else was going.

He was afoot in a field of sun-yellowed grass which had been trampled flat by thousands of feet. The crowd made no sense. Young and old, middle-aged and senior citizen, babes in arms, long-hairs and straights. A shirt-sleeve crowd, dogs yipping in the dust, transistor radios blaring country music.

Country music? He'd been shucked for sure. Sanders wouldn't be caught dead in this sort of hick crowd.

The mass was funneling down into a sluggish river of elbow-to-elbow humanity which flowed toward a central destination—a massive canvas tent pitched near the racetrack.

Carnival? No trucks or wagons, no midway, no barkers. But the other possibilities were almost endless. Rodeo? Boxing card? Tent revival? Country-western music show? Old-fashioned bam dance? Cattle auction or livestock judging? He seemed to be the only one in ignorance of which it was. Ah. Posters. But the crush of people was so immense that O'B couldn't see what the posters said. Everyone except him was excited, up, hyper, full of anticipation.

Inside at last, and not even an admission charge collected. Nothing but a portable wooden stage set up at one end of the vast canvas structure and a sea of folding chairs rapidly filling with people. No trapezes slung high overhead. No center rings for performing dogs or horses. No pens, no judging blocks for cattle.

And no Colonel Sanders.

O'B prowled and looked. A group of youngsters in white gowns with gold collars took their place on the wooden risers to the rear of the stage. They started singing "That Old Time Religion." He remembered, vividly and abruptly, sneaking under the canvas of revival tent shows as a kid. The Holy Rollers one year.

One big roll and save your soul.

He'd clapped erasers for a week after school at Mission High for chanting *that* one in the hall.

Tonight it was a good old fundamentalist preacher all in black urging the sinful to save their souls, wash themselves free from all sin, find God, testify to the Power of The Word.

O'B turned to go. It had been a ploy on Colonel Sanders' part to throw off any possible tail. Carefully skirting the traffic going to the tent revival, leaving O'B hopelessly mired in the jam-up. O'B's only edge was the pencil mike. Sanders wouldn't know about that. Once he and his blonde got going in that motel room—

The preacher had begun exhorting now, cajoling, arms thrust wide to gather in the sinful, his sweat flying, his voice hoarsening as it began to draw its inevitable emotional response.

"He hath filled the hungry with good things. Am I right?"

"You are right!" answered some voices from the crowd.

"He hath sent the rich away empty. Am I right?"

"You are *right!*"

O'B was working his way toward the exit to the parking lots.

"And I say to you, brethren, that The Shepherd rejoices more in the return of one lost sheep than he does in maintaining the whole flock. *Am I right?*"

"You are right!" With him now, a massive chorus.

"Then bring me your poor, and your maimed, and your halt, and your blind. And I will make them whole again. So saith the Lord. Brethren, *am I right?*"

"YOU ARE RIGHT!"

Now O'Bannon was breasting a tide—the old and the crippled and the sinful, moving down the aisle to bear witness to the Lord. He paused, looked back, and was transfixed. There, among them, was the familiar silver hair, the pain-lined ascetic face, the bobbing crabwise movement. O'B gaped.

Colonel Buford Sanders, angle-player and game-player and insurance defrauder, going down the aisle of a tent preacher's—

That's when the images began to flick before O'Bannon's eyes, frame after frame like a slide show. Images created from a blazing, belated, but now total comprehension.

Sanders, hiring *his own* private eye. Not a second tail on Sanders that Wednesday—*a tail on O'B!* And, later, a tail on Ballard. Identifying them, clocking their movements, habits.

So Sanders could pay his maid to stage a seduction scene for Ballard, after she had hung around Jacques Daniels' to make sure he would notice her.

Sanders, street-parking his Caddy where he knew O'B would spot it, once O'B believed Sanders was sneaking out of town at five a.m.

Sanders deliberately being too difficult to tail for suspicions to be aroused, but never so difficult that the tail could be lost.

Sanders maybe even paying the management to gimmick the air conditioner and shower in the room whoever was tailing him would be sure to rent. Playing games, as usual.

And Sanders playing *more* games—the non-incriminating phone call to the blonde when he *knew* his room would be bugged.

And now Sanders, head bowed beneath the hands of the Healer in a revival tent at the Santa Clara County fairgrounds, under the watchful eyes of 20,000 people.

"Oh, God!" cried the Colonel in a loud voice. *"Oh, God, I am saved! Oh, God be praised! Oh, see me, a sinner, SAVED!"*

And he cavorted around on the stage, shouting the power of the Lord, and hurled up the aisle at a certain red-haired man the cane he would never need again—as 20,000 throats roared their hysterical approval.

Oh, yes, the cane he would never need again. Because Colonel Buford Sanders, USAF, Ret'd, was $275,000 richer with no possibility of ever being charged with fraud. Some 20,000 good souls, and a trained detective besides, had witnessed the miracle of his cure. A trained detective who, under oath, could only testify as to what he had seen and heard. Who, indeed, had been carefully lured there for that very purpose.

It was too much. It was all just too damned much.

The Colonel embraced the Healer with tears of joy running down his face. As O'B had no doubt, he soon would embrace his blonde—with no worries about what a pencil mike from the next room might pick up.

O'B started to curse. Aloud.

Then the king said to the attendants, "Bind his hands and feet and cast him forth into the darkness outside . . ."

Yes, O'B cursed. Loudly and bitterly and blasphemously, from the very core of his soul, at how thoroughly and totally he had been set up and taken in by the Colonel. O'Bannon, the Unbeliever, cursed.

. . . where there shall be weeping and gnashing of teeth.

And they threw O'B out. Bodily.